Awesome

a novel by Jack Pendarvis

ALSO BY JACK PENDARVIS

The Mysterious Secret of the Valuable Treasure

Your Body Is Changing

Awesome

a novel by Jack Pendarvis

with illustrations by Michael Mitchell

MACADAM CAGE

MacAdam/Cage
155 Sansome Street, Suite 550
San Francisco, CA 94104
www.MacAdamCage.com

Library of Congress Cataloging-in-Publication Data

Pendarvis, Jack, 1963-
  Awesome : a novel / by Jack Pendarvis.
      p. cm.
  ISBN 978-1-59692-240-2
  1. Giants—Fiction. I. Title.
PS3616.E535A97 2008
813'.6—dc22

                                    2007050800

Portions of this novel originally appeared in *American Short Fiction*,
Hot Metal Bridge, and *The Yalobusha Review*.

Cover illustration by Michael Mitchell
Book design by Dorothy Carico Smith

Printed in the United States of America
1 2 3 4 5 6 7 8 9 10

For Theresa Starkey, Tom Franklin,
Mark Childress, and Jeff McNeil

And with thanks to John and Renee Grisham
and the University of Mississippi,
where I was allowed to finish the final draft at
my leisure as the visiting writer-in-residence

I think we've really been feeling awesome for four years.

—Céline Dion

／

Man, I look fantastic in this derby. Everybody's saying, Who's the dude in the derby?

It's so natural to me, I don't even realize I have it on. I'm just walking around. If people can't handle my derby, that's their problem.

Hey, we live in modern times these days. That derby doesn't fit into my view of the world, they silently complain. To which I reply, Exactly.

I'm going to go to that restaurant and show the girls my derby.

It's breakfast time. I'll have champagne to start off with. Hello, girls. I'm not going to mention my derby.

This is one of those restaurants where they hire waitresses

with a certain affronted poise. Black t-shirts, black jeans. Willowy. One of those restaurants. Goat cheese.

A sunshiny patio.

The latter must be cleared of both customers and tables so that I may have room to eat. Trees must be shorn of their branches. The awning is rolled up and stored to accommodate my height.

Hello. Will you tell me your name? Janette? Janette, you have a smile as big as all outdoors. Seraphic. There's a word, seraphic, that applies to you. You're like one of the seraphim, do you know what that is? It's a kind of an angel. Janette, I'll start off with a crate of champagne, thank you.

Why thank you, Janette. This omelet looks delicious. Janette, can you guess my name? You'll never guess. It's Mama Junior. I'm a man, but I'm named after my mama. She called me Mama Junior.

Janette? Janette? Guess what. I'm pulling your leg.

That was a great breakfast. I'm stuffed. I'll leave Janette a five percent tip.

2

I am a hale man with beautiful teeth. My doctor always remarks upon my superb physiognomy. I am strong and clean. This morning I put on a nice yellow shirt and some brown slacks, pleasant to the touch. I capped myself off with my lustrous derby.

Finder of lost kittens, fixer of potholes, I stride the sidewalks. I am a white American male of Scandinavian descent. I try to be a good citizen. I have all the money I will ever need. I go around seeing what I can do to help. I can lift an automobile if I have to. I can run fast. I am at ease with the lingo of the common folk, explaining complex truths in a down-to-earth slang accessible to all. I can leap one hundred yards from a standstill, if necessary. I have the skills to build a robot. Deep down I am just a regular guy.

I am a giant. My name is AWESOME.

3

Here is a normal day for me.

Wake up.

Look at my handsome nakedness in my big mirror.

My robot ward, Jimmy, is already up and making coffee. I could turn Jimmy into a wife robot if I wanted to. I could stretch him out to giant size and add some female-looking parts and a sluice of some kind where I could deposit my ejaculate. I could give him a different voice and name and put some eyelashes on him. But it wouldn't seem right.

Aside from dining, sleeping, and a few other biological necessities,

I strive to divide each day of my life into four exactly equal parts, comprised of, respectively, meditation, recreation, industry, and avocation.

⌐

Meditation takes many forms. It begins when I catch the morning bus with the regular people. Technically, I pick up the bus and carry it downtown. Everyone seems to enjoy the change of pace. When I have arrived I generally stare at the fountain.

I might invent a religion, or make mental notations for my dream journal. These may be records of dreams I have had, or speculations upon dreams I expect to have in the future.

Examples:

Dream of a series of moustaches.

Dream of a father-in-law with a thin, forked sexual member listless on his chin.

Dream of magma.

Dream of a glass bubble half filled with explosive powder.

The aquarium is nearby. Its high ceilings I find appealing. I can crawl through the wide front doors and move about in a comfortable crouch.

Meditation may involve contemplating the beluga whale. He radiates in a key sympathetic to my own. Everybody's saying, Check out that dude looking at the whale. Do they have some kind of freaky mind meld going on or what?

In their own way, my admirers are on to something.

There is a large viewing area, like a dance floor. When I sit there, there is not much room left over. The others don't mind. They crowd around as best they can, enjoying my connection with the beluga whale.

The beluga whale twirls in the water.

The beluga whale is patched with rough disease. He has a scar indicating emasculation. Overall, however, his skin could be made into a nice suitcase, possibly the nicest suitcase ever manufactured.

His eye is intelligent and probing. When he rubs against the glass his skin becomes smooth and flat like rubber, plastic, or ice cream. He possesses gorgeous, supple leg-like muscles where his legs would be, were he to have legs. His leg muscles seem to validate the theory of evolution in a wholesome way. He is playful. He blows a kind of spit bubble, a water ring, which floats in front of his face for a moment before he swallows it. A recreational game. The varieties of twirling, swimming, floating, spinning, and whirling he demonstrates are slow and limitless. His value as an object of meditation is likewise slow and limitless.

The beluga whale, says the guide, was rescued from somewhere. He enjoys people as much as people enjoy him. He has a life expectancy of fifty. His skin disease is in the process of healing. Where he was rescued, the water was too warm. He prefers the icy arctic climes. Any questions.

I raise my hand and ask the guide his name. Steven? I had a cousin named Steven. He was killed in basic training. You're so lucky, Steven. You have a wonderful head of hair. Is it naturally curly? People seem soothed by you. How about it, everybody? Don't you find Steven soothing? You're on top of your whale information. I have complete trust that I could ask you anything about a whale and you would know the answer. That's a rare gift, I hope you don't ever forget it. I know you won't. You're a special person, Steven.

In a way, Steven, yes, that is a question about the whale.

6

Recreation is subdivided into three-fourths aiding and one-fourth joshing.

Aiding is reserved for strangers in need.

Aiding is further subdivided into three-fifths active and two-fifths passive.

Active aiding is sub-sub-subdivided into one-half physical aid, one-half mental/spiritual aid.

As an example of mental/spiritual aid, consider my conversation with Steven, the aquarium guide, who had hairs growing *on* his nose, not just in it. I imagine that he had, on more than one occasion, applied a safety razor to those unusual surface hairs, and that as a result, they had grown back thicker each time, getting him down in the dumps.

It should be noted that the conversation is subtracted from my meditation time and placed in the recreation file, under the appropriate aid column. Meditation, recreation, industry, and avocation are not scheduled as successive occupations, but may occur at any time of day, though never simultaneously. It does often happen that meditation comes early in the day, as a matter of personal preference and happenstance.

Example of passive aid: my derby.

When people see me wearing my derby they are filled with feelings they can't explain. Perhaps not all of these feelings are positive, at first blush. Jealousy and confusion, for example. Inability to accept things that are different. Worries about money. Will they ever have enough money to buy a derby like mine? Issues of self-esteem. I could never pull off a derby like that, is a sample thought. I don't have the face for it, the genes. Later, they go home and think about their feelings. At this point, negativity is turned into learning and growing.

Joshing may occur with friends or strangers, such as the waitress Janette. Joshing, if continued over a period of time, will turn a stranger into a friend.

As an example of my industry, I may cite the time a university asked me to construct two robots for use in a robot debate. The project was a joint venture of the science and philosophy departments and the divinity school.

I programmed one robot's brain with the works of David Hume. His friend I programmed with the works of Emanuel Swedenborg.

The first robot, set to shuffle mode, opened the debate with a reference to the second book of Hume's *A Treatise of Human Nature*, entitled "Of the Passions." Drawing on Section 12, *Of the pride and humility of animals*, subsection 4, he proved through a system of rationality that turkeys are haughty and snobbish, while nightingales are proud of their singing abilities.

My second robot retorted, making use of part 108 of Swedenborg's *De Coelo et ejus mirabilibus, et de Inferno, ex auditis et visis*, that bees, caterpillars, and birds, lacking rationality, are closer to the Divine path than man.

Having served their purpose, the robots were dismantled, a process to which each submitted peaceably.

Avocation: Alpine bells.

After all the good I try to do it seems a small thing to ask that I be given the liberty to spend a fourth of every day (minus sleep, etc.) playing songs on my Alpine bells. My downstairs neighbor Glorious Jones has had a problem with it in the past. I've received several notes of complaint, and once she called the police.

The police officers were hearty men of good cheer. We had hot chocolate. Before the evening was done I had taught them to play a few simple tunes with my Alpine bells. They stomped on the floor as they danced and played. My downstairs neighbor came up to see what all the commotion was about:

Can't you see this is driving me crazy. I'm restoring a mosaic.

I explained how the Alpine bells clear the system of all its woes. I suggested that with her large wet eyes, tattered shift, and unkempt blue-black hair she resembled a delightful urchin. I hinted that if police officers could make the best of the Alpine bells, so could anyone. I invited her to join in. I shook the bell on my left hand. I shook the bell on my left leg. I shook the bell on my enormous, pendant member.

My downstairs neighbor was filled with wonder.

Is that what I think it is.

Yes, it is an Alpine bell.

It's inhumanly large.

You're welcome to give it a tinkle.

My downstairs neighbor and the two policemen went to work on my Alpine bell. Due to friction and other scientific factors, the member to which the bell was attached reached its maximum girth and extension, roughly the size of the largest Kodiak bear on record springing forward to protect her innocent cubs from nefarious poachers. The resultant release of ejaculate, two hours and twenty minutes later, shattered one of my front windows and hit the power lines outside. There was an explosion, and the neighborhood was plunged into darkness.

My capacity for love is unbounded. My exuberance requires placation twelve times every day. Ejaculatory release, like sleeping and dining, falls under the rubric of necessity, and subtracts significantly from the total hours I am able to devote to the four key areas of my daily routine.

My schedule, as you can see, is a taxing one. The concentration involved would cause an ordinary person's brain to crumble into bits like a Renaissance fresco or a muffin. As a precaution, I treat myself to an annual vacation lasting ten months.

During my yearly ten-month vacation, I perform meditative, recreational, industrial, and avocational activities in any combination I please, or not at all.

Here is the usual way in which my vacation commences:

I post flyers in the quads near the humanities departments of regional universities, seeking young men and women for special companionship.

We load into the car—myself, my robot ward, Jimmy, and the six females and two males I have chosen based on their written applications and an intensive series of interviews and psychological profiling.

The car is built to hover or float over the other traffic. It would not be fair to take up the eight lanes of interstate my marvelous car would require.

The car is of my own design, and is fueled by my ejaculate.

My member is fitted into a Plexiglas tube. My helpers work in two-person teams for six-hour shifts, insuring a regular flow of fresh ejaculate into the reserve tanks. I am capable of driving for seventy-two hours at a time. I then sleep for twenty-four to thirty-six hours while my robot ward, Jimmy, takes over the driving. I have ordinarily produced upwards of fifty gallons of ejaculate, more than enough to fuel the car for 6,200 miles of travel. We stop only to buy homemade jellies from quaint roadside fruit stands or snap photos with our iPhones of billboards containing humorous grammatical errors and/or unintentional double entendres, the latter of which I intend to self-publish in an eight-volume collector's edition with slipcase.

That, as I said, is the usual way, but this year's vacation was to be a honeymoon.

I had chosen to marry my downstairs neighbor, Glorious Jones, in a ceremony of my own devising, based upon a religion I had invented one morning at the fountain.

The ceremony began with the performance of an oratorio entitled *The Doomed Waif*, which I had composed on the preceding afternoon. Representatives of a book company approached me on the morning of my wedding, hoping to include me in a record book for having attained the world's record for composing an oratorio in the quickest amount of time.

I asked them not to sully my wedding day with commerce. When they insisted that I deserved an especial accolade for my work, I picked them up in my arms (there were five of them) and tossed them into the treetops, where they could be heard protesting until the commencement of the overture, the beauty of which struck them dumb with pleasure. I believe they discovered that riches and awards are no match for art. Two of them later died of their injuries. A third expired from joy.

I will skip over most of the details of the ceremony, which was esoteric, hermetic, and arcane to such a degree that even those who witnessed it were incapable of describing it afterward.

For the inevitably curious I can confirm that, yes, I did wear my derby.

I could feel the eyes of the wedding guests on me, marveling. When the time came for me to acquiesce to the union I revealed to the delight of all present that I had written my own vows.

Glorious Jones, I recited, you're a truly gifted and accomplished person and a great beauty of your kind, in your small, peculiar category. No one can take that away from you. It isn't your fault that your looks wither next to mine, wither into humiliating rot. Indeed, that only makes me love you more. For what is more important than achievement and beauty in this strange world? I will tell you. Bravery. The first time I noticed your bravery was when you answered my ad in the newspaper and appeared to have no qualms about living below me, on the first floor of the magnificent brownstone specially constructed so that a man of my particulars might live and work at ease. Perhaps it was the cheap rent that enticed you. Or perhaps it was your bravery. Because, as the fine print in your lease pointed out, you daily faced the prospect of an unfortunate crushing, or being deafened by my footsteps overhead, like unto thunder, or suffering any number of long-term medical problems due to the radiation emanating from my robots. And many times you violated your rental agreement, such as the part about not cooking food with terrible smelling spices. And I found it in my overflowing heart to forgive you. For you are what is called a normal woman. But by marrying me, Glorious Jones, you have shown yourself to be the bravest woman of all, and I suppose it could be proven that doing something like that is a kind of weird beauty, even if it doesn't count by most standards. A lot of the time, stuff that's not supposed to count ends up being important, and everybody's like, Wow, I didn't see that coming. So congratulations. Congratulations upon your nuptial day.

Even though everybody here is probably thinking that you're the lucky one, because I am a wildly attractive and powerful giant and everything, I invite them to come back in sixty years or so. I don't age much, so you'll most likely be mistaken for my great-grandmother or something. But your inner beauty by that time will be resplendent, and that's apparently what really counts, so good for you. You've already got a real head start, baby, no kidding. Isn't she a peach, folks? Now, without any further ado, let's get it on, Glorious Jones. That's right, start peeling. [At this point the camel came out.] Let's hop on the camel I rented as a special surprise and do it on camelback in front of everybody, for then they will have witnessed the essence of true love. Actually, you will have to pleasure yourself on camelback while I watch from on high in the company of all our friends and your agéd mother, whom we are so pleased to have with us here today, because I could totally kill that camel by accident with nothing more than my pinkie finger. In fact, I'm going to have to ask the bridesmaids, and whoever else wants to chip in, to help me out with my part of the consummation, for as you well know, it is not a job for one man. I know we have been discussing how we might do it together, just you and me, and I have been thinking of instating a contest on the internet with a million-dollar prize for the scientist, philosopher, or gifted amateur who comes up with the solution prior to your inevitable decline. But for today, it just ain't happening, to put it in layman's terms that all our wedding guests can understand. Papa needs lots of extra help. Still, all the time I will be looking at you, baby. Looking at you for the eternity of our married lives, no matter what kind of freaky stuff is going down in my pants. Okay, I see that the camel is getting antsy. Get cracking, Glorious Jones, show everybody what you've got down there, and what you can make it do, and this wedding ceremony I invented with my brain will come to its astounding conclusion.

There was a small hush as many fainted from my eloquence and others from the prospect of being pressed into the holiest of conjugal services.

But what about the vows *I* wrote? said Glorious Jones.

That wasn't really part of the plan, sweetheart, I said. Not that I'm not completely delighted at the prospect, but it does throw a kink into the schedule. So maybe we should skip it.

I'll make it quick, said Glorious Jones. She proceeded to defame me in the foulest language imaginable, concluding with the statement that she wouldn't marry me if I were the last person on the bleeping earth. Using a grappling hook that I had intended for the dramatic finale of the ceremony, she sprang to a nearby rooftop and made what I can only call her escape.

Jimmy, my robot ward, conducted a quick chemical analysis of two tiny dots of moisture adorning the silken runner athwart which Glorious Jones had erstwhile stood. He found them to be composed of a saline compound not incompatible with the makeup of actual human tears.

Yes, there was a 98.5% certainty that I had made Glorious Jones cry. I blamed my passion for complex prose.

I struck the ground again and again with my mighty fists until a sinkhole opened up, swallowing the wedding guests. I flooded the sinkhole with my copious tears, enabling most of those trapped therein to float to the surface and escape unharmed.

As twilight approached I found myself alone in the shambles I had made of the botanical gardens, the intended site of my connubial union. How many harmless trees had I uprooted, how many innocent flowers plucked asunder? How many Japanese bridges had I chewed into splinters? How many swans had I terrified? What had I done to the camel?

I am not by nature a destructive dude. I prefer to chill out, live and let live, whatever turns you on. As long as we're not hurting each other I don't see how it's any of the government's business what we do behind closed doors.

But part of rationality lies in recognizing our own propensity to freak out at the drop of a hat. Perhaps I had performed a miracle of a kind, resisting the urge as long as I had. The downside was that a freak-out thrown by a person of my strengths and abilities could result in the desolation of the great cities of the earth. Maybe I would have been able to calm down of my own free will. Or maybe I was fooling myself, which was why the emergency plan had been instituted.

This was not a drill.

Step One: Walk to the Great Lakes region. Given my special powers and singleness of purpose, I was able to accomplish this task before sunset. I admit I was walking westward, which afforded me an advantage as I crossed time zones.

By special prearrangement between myself and the Department of Homeland Security, the Coast Guard had set up a secret base, the sole purpose of which was to monitor Lake Ontario for signs of my approach.

The moment I took off my pants (but left on my shoes, for reasons which will soon be clear) and waded into the middle of the lake, a special submarine was dispatched. This remarkable vehicle—an exact replica of the one produced by H.L. Hunley for use in the Confederate Navy, save for one key factor—was piloted expertly by remote control into my anal cavity, where, in its capacity as a suppository, it began to dissolve. The submarine was composed of (in lieu of the traditional boiler iron) a powerful tranquilizer of my own invention. The effects of the drug were immediate, and it was all I could do to drag myself out of the water.

Step Two: An entire jamboree of Boy Scouts was parachuted in. As I stood half dozing they tied my shoelaces together into one massive knot of unimaginable complexity—a knot unrecorded in any Boy Scout manual, I might mention, the secret of which is to be handed down orally from generation to generation of Eagle Scouts in rituals of dark and threatening solemnity. The knot, like the tranquilizer, was of my own design. I had performed surgery on myself to remove the part of my brain where the method for untying the knot was stored, in anticipation of events like the ones related heretofore.

12

Even tranquilized and handicapped by a self-applied partial lobotomy, I was a whiz at untying knots. As my head cleared and the gray, furry world came into focus, I discovered that I had been applying myself to the task for a number of hours even in my slumber, like the go-getter that I knew myself to be. Enthused by this self-affirmation, I concentrated on the job at hand, making an enjoyable game of it. By the time I had unlaced my shoes and retrieved my pants I was in my usual placid frame of mind.

I dawdled on the long walk back to my home state, noticing the characteristics of birds and other classy things.

I confess that as I walked I allowed myself to think that Glorious Jones had cooled down as well, and would be waiting to patch things up.

But our home had been emptied of her things. It had been emptied of my things as well. All my important experiments and inventions had been wiped from the earth as if they had never existed.

Jimmy, my robot ward, had arrived home just before me, or so he said.

Where have you been, Jimmy? You're not programmed to go places and do things. Your homing device should have sent you here directly after the ceremony. Part of your job is being on the lookout for intruders and industrial competitors.

I was at the mall, said Jimmy, my robot ward. I was trying to win you a pickup truck in a radio contest to make you feel better.

That makes no sense for a number of reasons, Jimmy.

You should get the police on her ass, said Jimmy, my robot ward, a sweeping motion of his robot arm indicating the emptiness all about us. He was speaking of Glorious Jones.

I hardly think that's necessary. A wedding is the best day of a girl's life, and there's a lot of unfair pressure built up around it. It would be unusual *not* to get the jitters.

That's no excuse to treat you like dirt, said Jimmy, my robot ward. If she comes slinking back you should tell her to hit the bricks.

There's one possible miscalculation that has been nagging at me, Jimmy. You specifically tabulated a 92% probability that Glorious Jones's most deeply held fantasy was doing it on a camel in public. Could you run a quick scan on that math for me?

Let's go bowling first, said Jimmy, my robot ward.

I have to stick around here, Jimmy. Glorious Jones might call.

Put me on the phone. I'll tell her right where she can go.

Someone knocked at the door.

This might be her, I said, shoving Jimmy into the closet.

My visitor introduced himself as Glorious Jones's attorney, Hap Martin. He was a skeletal young man, his almost fully receded hair of a paleness described by Lord Byron in his famous poem about dudes kicking back in a dungeon. His moustache, however, was eloquent—of the pencil-thin variety and fussed over a great deal. His eyes were as dead as lost buttons, his teeth and ears on the pointy side. He wore a black cape lined with royal purple and used a walking stick topped with a silver wolf's head.

I have papers, he said. My client has requested that you sign them in blood.

On one condition. I must speak to her.

I'm afraid that is impossible, said her attorney, Hap Martin.

Well then, just tell her there are no hard feelings about cleaning out the brownstone. It was totally within her rights. She knows that everything I have is hers.

My client did not partake in any such unauthorized confiscation of your goods, sir. I can only assume that you have hidden your assets in anticipation of the inevitable court decision against you.

I assure you that my robot ward, Jimmy, came home to find the living quarters in their present condition. His heat sensors detected an afterglow in the exact shape of Glorious Jones, or so he has informed me. And he is a reliable machine.

May I remind the gentleman that Glorious Jones is no machine, but a refined and talented lady of real flesh and blood?

While your description is undoubtedly accurate in a technical sense, I fail to see its bearing on our current conversation. Putting that aside, however, at least may I know: Is there any chance that Glorious Jones will take me back?

To my surprise, attorney Hap Martin ripped his legal documents into quarters.

With your voluntary posing of that question, sir, I have been authorized to give you this.

He withdrew from his shirt pocket a packet of letters in lavender envelopes, tied round about with a silver riband of shimmeringest gossamer. A faint waft of gardenia greeted me, the preferred scent of Glorious Jones.

I reached for these blessed reminders but with a lawyerly trick Hap Martin snatched them away.

Ah, ah, ah, he said. You are to open one envelope at a time, starting with the topmost of the packet. With each envelope you open, an object of your quest will be revealed to you. You are not to open another envelope before finding the present object. When you have opened the last envelope and found the final object, Miss Jones will consider that you have done your penance and proven your love. At that time, you will be allowed to meet her face to face, state the reasons for your past behavior, beg for her forgiveness, and make a case for whatever future relationship with her that you deem probable at that juncture.

So if I succeed at a simple scavenger hunt, I win back the trust and love of Glorious Jones, I summarized.

I am young but precocious and experienced, said Hap Martin. In my many years at the bench I have locked horns with perhaps a score of worthy foes. May I say that you have proven to be the most eloquent and insightful of them all. It has been a true pleasure to match wits with you, sir. And so I leave you with this bit of advice: Beware. Things are often more complicated than they seem.

I have never found that to be the case, I said. But I thank you for your input.

Hap Martin vanished in an eructation of malodorous brown smoke.

13

Setting off on foot, alone, without my robot ward, Jimmy, without my special car or collegiate helpers, full of ejaculate which I had no desire to dispense, in the plain, roughhewn clothing of a common day laborer and with nothing but my derby to remind me of the past, I knew somehow that this would be a vacation like no other.

Who does he think he is with that terrific derby, I interpreted as the feelings of my observers. A derby like that belongs

on a titan, not this hulking vagrant with the grizzled beard and
hollow, downcast eyes.

Yes, my derby had become my crown of thorns.

I was not leaping or hastening, and many times I stopped and
shook my head at the pointlessness of scenery. It was about
four-thirty in the afternoon when I made it to the edge of town.
There was a high school there, and probably not the town's best
one, given its remote location. Some grossly pustular members
of the rugby team, greasy bangs hanging in their eyes, made
rude noises at me as I passed, noises that I recall as chicky
chicky chicky chicky and yah yah yah.

I ignored them and continued walking. The problems of
our nation's teenagers were the last thing on my mind. I had not
yet opened the envelope that would determine the first item of
my hunt, and the curiosity teased at me, but the time didn't feel
right, nor the place. So I walked and wandered. The teenagers,
meantime, exalted with endorphins and testosterone, flushed
with youthful high spirits, driven by the herd mentality, blinded
by societal conceptions of manliness, instinctively drawn
toward the forgotten initiatory rites of decimated civilizations,
pursued me into a thicket, where they pounded me without
mercy. I did not toss them into the treetops as I might have
done on any other day. I let them kick me back and forth in the

muck as best they could. Their blows were ineffective, but I rolled and grunted a bit, trying to understand how it would feel to be abused and punished. I was roused only when one of them threatened, in his words, to pinch a loaf in my fancy hat.

O God, is this what has become of beauty?

I roared. My voice blew a black wind that bent the elms. My young tormentors scattered in every direction. The sky grew dark all at once, and it began to hail.

15

When I awoke in the thicket the night was deep and clear. The frogs made agreeable noises. By some luck, my derby was covering my face, and had endured the worst of the storm.

16

I made it across the county line, where I recognized the towers of an opulent hotel from the bridal brochures that Glorious Jones had scattered about her workspace.

I approached, bending low to greet the doorman.

Good evening, sir, he said, his walrus moustache fringed with nicotine.

Could you tell me, please, whether there is an entranceway through which I might fit? A loading dock perhaps?

Hmm, could be, he said, holding out his hand in the

familiar fashion.

I crossed his palm with gulden.

Nope, come to think of it, there's not, he said.

That's very odd. I was supposed to stay here on my honeymoon night and no one indicated that it would be a problem. I made special inquiries. May I speak with a manager?

Well, I could go get him, but who would watch the door? Would you want me to be fired?

He held out his hand again. I obliged him and he went inside, returning a few moments later, alone.

Sorry, the manager's not here, he said. Who you want is the night manager, I suppose.

And might he be fetched? I inquired.

He might, the doorman replied, holding out his hand.

I gave him twice as much money as before. He seemed happy to see it, rattling the doubloons together then biting them in his teeth, one after the other. But when he returned again, he explained that the night manager had suffered a seizure and was lying down in an unoccupied room with a cool cloth on his forehead.

Who is in charge in the night manager's absence? I asked.

The bell captain, he replied.

Another display of munificence produced this grand figure, dressed head to toe in a flattering uniform of red and gold, cut tight and attractive around the haunches.

The bell captain was efficient and sympathetic. He told me of a local tourist attraction, a cathedral several miles up the road, with which the hotel enjoyed a good working relationship.

We send a lot of foot traffic their way, he said. I believe we can arrange for you to sleep there tonight. There will be a surcharge, of course, payable in cash.

Superstition and magic don't make it with me. In layman's terms, I don't dig the guilt rap that the pope and a few other ornery dudes are laying down on the ordinary joe, who just wants to take off his work boots and pop open a cold one in front the boob tube.

Yet before entering the cathedral, which was of recent vintage though constructed in the medieval style, I removed my derby and hung it on the central bell tower, not as a matter of deference, but out of simple comfort and plain good manners.

I cracked a couple of pillars squeezing my shoulders through, but the doors themselves were welcoming and abundant.

Once inside I could stand up and stretch quite easily. I would estimate that the ceiling was well over one hundred feet high, affording me ample headroom, and the nave resembled an immense warehouse, its transepts not much more than nubs. Of course there were smaller chapels I could not enter, but I put my cheek to the cool stone floor and looked inside and they were very pretty from an aesthetic point of view even though I did not agree with what they represented.

I was wakened at sunrise by a light sensation of tickling about my calves, not unpleasant. I discerned at once several gaunt priests attacking me with brooms, rakes, and pitchforks.

I explained that I had squared things with the bell captain, but they continued to prod and poke me.

I wriggled out of the front doors as best I could, but in my haste I am afraid there was further damage to the superstructure.

I would be glad to pay for that, I said. If someone could fetch my clothes, which I folded neatly and stored beneath the pews in the quire, my wallet is inside.

I saw that the priests had already pressed several hardy altar boys into service, a cadre of whom was engaged in forcing my coveralls out the doors and into a pile at my feet.

I dressed quickly and reached for my derby.

It was gone.

I guess you think you're getting my goat by hiding my most prized possession, I said. Well, I have news for you. Possessions don't mean much in this crazy world. Church isn't a building. Like, I could walk around in the grass with my shoes off and totally feel like I was in a church.

I could see that the priests were rethinking their position.

Like, this dude we hit with brooms has just given me the best sermon I have ever heard. I wasted a ton of money on seminary and here this guy just comes up with it off the top of his head.

I should thank you for taking away my derby, I said. Maybe my hair is all messed up, but maybe that's how I want it to look. Maybe that's a casual look that people are really going for right now. Maybe you've helped me rather than hurt me. Maybe you're not such bad guys after all. Maybe you've produced the circumstance under which I have come to the end of my evasions.

It was true: there was nothing else to do. I was divested of my luxuries, which I now saw as impediments. I had no awesome derby, no roof wide enough to shelter me, no magnificent brownstone built to my mighty scale and filled with designer sheets, tawny port, and vintage pinball machines. As deferential menservants receded and vanished, only con men and charlatans came forward to fill the gaps. I had only one thing left to believe in. I withdrew from the pouch of my workmanlike burlap overalls the gardenia-scented stationery filled with secrets.

I pulled upon the delicate knot and the riband fell aside, releasing its sweet and portentous cargo. I removed the topmost envelope and tied the rest of the envelopes together again, precisely as I had found them.

I broke the glued flap, glue that had held fast, perhaps, through the auspices of the precious spittle of Glorious Jones.

I withdrew the simple slip of pellucid lavender tucked within. There I found a message in her excellent and distinctive calligraphy:

A NEEDLE IN A HAYSTACK

20

How does one find a needle in a haystack? The very term opens up a whole slew of ethical and epistemological questions, such as, how small may my stack be and still be called a haystack? May I put the needle into the haystack myself? Does this exercise require first finding a haystack that has previously had a needle legitimately lost in it, that is, by mistake? Or may the needle be hidden in the haystack on purpose? If I hire someone to hide the needle in the haystack, have I really found a needle in a haystack? Even if I locate the needle under the latter circumstance, I have created the conditions under which the needle might be found. Such an action would violate the spirit of any scavenger hunt—as if I were asked to find a red dress, went to my closet, took out a white dress, bought some red dye, dyed the white dress red, and claimed that I just found a red dress.

Nor do the complications end there.

Assuming I do find a haystack containing a previously lost needle, may I remove some of the hay in order to find it? Then, of course, it is no longer a haystack, and if I find the needle, it won't be in a haystack, but in what I may call a non-stack, or unstack. How much hay might I disturb before a haystack stops being a haystack?

Glorious Jones had issued a serious challenge and I intended to meet it in spirit and letter, so that there could be no question of my commitment to her merest wish.

First, obviously, I needed to find the town in which it was most likely that a needle might already be lying there lost in a haystack.

It couldn't be a town known for sweatshops, clothing factories, or other industrial seamstress work. Men and women employed at such labor would not likely take their needles out of the factory and into the fields. At the end of a working day they would wish to put as much distance between themselves and their needles as possible. I needed to locate a hub of recreational sewing—in the form, say, of sewing circles.

Knitting had really taken hold with today's modern kids. Graduate students got together and knitted to relieve themselves of stress. Glorious Jones had confirmed this trend for me, before the tragedy, during the time we used to lie in bed at four in the morning and talk about such things. Sometimes we would wake up in the middle of a conversation, or singing.

There were homemade zines, Glorious Jones had said, dedicated to the underground knitting culture. But I was not looking for a knitting needle in a haystack, though the challenge was not specific as to the type of needle to be found. A knitting needle would be as far from the spirit of the quest as a hypodermic needle, or the Seattle Space Needle, which would easily poke out of an average haystack, though I suppose a large enough haystack could be constructed, perhaps a haystack as large as the state of Washington, rising into the stratosphere, though even then a simple Global Positioning System would render the search an indolent and useless one. The whole meaning of the phrase needle in a haystack pivots upon the image of a tiny silver needle, no longer than one and a half inches, the kind of needle with an eye so small you have to wet the end of the thread to make it fit, the kind of needle Jesus was talking about that time.

Hay is, indeed, for horses.

Using my preexisting knowledge of American geography, bestowed on me by the excellent prep schools of my youth, I recalled that Kentucky is known for both its horses and protein-rich grasses (not many people know that its official nickname even comes from a type of grass, bluegrass) perfect for making hay. I had read a dryly humorous account in the Escapes section of the *New York Times* about a renowned quilting bee in the town of _____, a bee which had been going on, non-stop, since 1893. The quilts produced in said bee are famed for their intricate stitching. Here, then, in _____, Kentucky, needle was bound to meet haystack.

It took me forty-five minutes to walk to Kentucky, and by walking I mean a series of superhuman leaps interspersed with extremely fast running and, when the wind proved conducive, something approaching actual flight. Once in Kentucky, it took me five additional minutes to find the town of _____ by the process of elimination, a scientific trick of mine.

My wealth had always precluded me from much truck with the working class, but a large part of my recreation, during non-vacation months, consisted of going around and telling them they weren't as bad as they thought they were.

I had become able, in this way, to spot the haunts frequented by just the type of man who would toil in and around a haystack for a living. When I came to a tavern called the Rusty Hoe, I knew I had found the place to exist quietly among the farmers and pickers and such and eavesdrop until the inevitable subject of hay came up. With that opening, I would be able to sidle up and buy my newfound buddies a drink or two, meanwhile easing the conversation around to anyone who might have lost a needle in the vicinity of said hay, particularly in a stack of it. Best of all, the Rusty Hoe was roofless, so that I could step right in and mingle unobtrusively. To be precise, one of my shoes could fit in with no trouble at all, leaving plenty of navigating room all around it for any regular person who cared to join me. I had never attempted mingling before, and was titillated at the prospect. I felt certain that the distraction of my exceptional and enviable height and girth would be trumped by the homey, defeated demeanor I hoped to cultivate.

The interior of the Rusty Hoe happily exceeded my expectations. More squalid than I might have dreamt, it was just four walls and hardly anything to stand between a man and his drink. All over the dirt floor lay slimy pockets of tobacco which the occasional live chicken inspected for seeds. There was nobody home but the barkeep and an old woman in a bonnet and gingham dress, dead to the world, dipping snuff at the bar.

Such solitude was ideal for my purposes. By quitting time later that day, when the men of _____ left the fields and came looking for a drink, I would have managed to become an immutable part of the atmosphere, acceptable as one of their own.

As open and desolate as it was, the taproom provided cheer in two immediate aspects: first, the bright sunlight, which was perhaps too cheery for such an establishment, but seemed pleasantly conjoined with the heat of the potbellied stove; next, the cherrywood bar carved with mermaids, grapes, and roses.

I asked the barkeep for a washtub to be filled with vermouth and had him fetch sixteen large jars of pickled eggs and two of pickled pigs' feet from the basement. I was pleased to note that he treated me like any other customer, taking care to address me with a large cheerleader's megaphone and sending up the eggs and feet via a cleverly constructed standalone dumbwaiter. That he made these accommodations to my size so casually I marked down to my success at blending in, little suspecting at the time the true reason.

Before enjoying my refreshment, I tendered a friendly greeting toward the venerable old soul at the end of the bar, but she seemed to be living in a world of her own troubles, and did not respond.

The pastoral murmuring of the chickens and my soft, nearly noiseless sucking down of a whole jar of eggs at a time were disrupted by a boot which trod heavily on mine, containing a foot as large as my own.

This bar ain't big enough for the both of us, said the hairy behemoth attached to the foot.

It's not actually big enough for either of us, I observed.

This here is my spot, he said. Why, you've put your big foot right down in my natural footprint that I've a-spent so many years imprintin in this here floor. And them's my eggs you're a-chompin and a-eatin on so casual.

Easy, friend, I said. I'm just here in town because I'm an innocent haystack worker looking for a break.

His hair was black and curly and his beard was black and curly, so massive that it nearly hid his face. Black curly hair cascaded over the top button of his flannel shirt. He wore a wool hat and dungarees, and even his big black boots were covered in curly fur. He stuck out his chest and proclaimed:

My name is Goliath Brigadoon, and I'll lick any man here who says that round-balin ain't the most efficient way to bale hay.

To my surprise, the little old lady—who was only about seven feet tall—hopped off her stool, shot a gob of snuff on the floor, wiped her mouth on her gingham sleeve, and rebuked him:

I go by the name of Great Granny McPhee, and I been square-baling hay since before you was born. Why, if you mention round-baling again I'll make you eat them words afore this day is done.

Why, if you was a man, said Goliath Brigadoon, I'd twirl you over my head on one finger till your face turned blue, then I'd sling you in that corner over yonder, and while you was sittin there all dazed and bewildered I'd grab me a buzz saw sure as shootin and saw off the top of your head and dig out your brains. Then I reckon I'd jerk your head right up off of your neck-hole, and I'd commence to sealin up the bottom of your decapitated head with some kind of industrial sealant and ship it off to a novelty factory where they could make a souvenir stein out of it, hell, I'd send the top part, too, the flap of your skull, so's they could make one of them fancy steins out of it, to where you twiddle the little thingamabob and the lid flips up, and the lid I'm a-talkin and a-speakin about would be the top of your skull. Then I'd take the whole dad blame thing to one of them spots where you paint your own ceramics and I'd paint a picture of my cat Mr. Buttons on it, and boy wouldn't I have a swell time drinkin Ovaltine out of your skull. Seein as how you're a lady I won't do any of them terrible things I just mentioned, but I'm just sayin.

Now at what point did my dad blame decapitated head turn into a skull, supposedly, in this great world you've concocted with the fantasies of your rotten soul? said Great Granny McPhee.

At some point in the stein-makin process, roared Goliath Brigadoon.

Them's fighting words, said Great Granny McPhee.

She ran over and leapt up and down again and again, the better to slap Goliath Brigadoon around the anklebones with a paper funeral parlor fan.

Haw haw haw he laughed and bent down real close so she could slap him in the face with the paper fan.

Haw haw haw that don't hurt at all.

Our culture has not been taught to appropriately prize manliness and I sensed right away the profound psychological emasculation to which Goliath Brigadoon was being subjected. Great Granny McPhee had chosen, quite deftly, if inhumanely, to assault him with that most subtle and devastating of weapons:

her own weakness. How could he respond, aside from an ineffective haw haw haw? Hollow laughter, which masked a crumbling manhood.

I lifted Great Granny McPhee high in the air, and brought her down over my extended index finger, thereby cracking her spine like so much kindling.

Great Granny McPhee appeared to go into a coma. Her vital signs were negligible.

Stand back, I am a faith healer, said Goliath Brigadoon.

He knelt (destroying a wall of the bar, such was his beneficent haste) and breathed the breath of life into Great Granny McPhee. It appeared to be a pink smoke, which inflated her the way helium inflates a flat balloon. I made a mental note to check the leading medical journals for the appropriate scientific explanation.

Where the doodle am I? said the recovered Great Granny McPhee.

Git on out of here and tend to your hay, said the barkeep. I've had enough trouble for one day.

Great Granny McPhee sprang to her feet, as lithesome as a summer's lass, and flitted away.

Haw haw haw said Goliath Brigadoon. Let's see what kind of man breaks the back of a pore ole biddy. It's yore whuppin time, he informed me, his dialect congealing perceptibly.

See here my good man. I was only trying to help.

You've just boughten yoreself a wrasslin match.

So be it. Under one condition. If I win, you'll have to tell me everything you know about hay.

With that, we commenced our battle.

I got Goliath Brigadoon into my patented chokehold. He broke several of his jagged teeth attempting to bite through my impenetrable arm, which is as hard as any diamond. One of his incisors, however, became lodged and snapped off in my soft, downy navel, my area of vulnerability. Who knew what communicable diseases wriggled invisible on the surface of that loathsome denticle?

I gave Goliath Brigadoon a kick that sent him hopping. He smashed the front of the tavern, clattered across the alley, and broke through the back of a place where you go to paint your own ceramics. After smashing every dish, pot, and cream pitcher, he rolled onto the Main Street of _____, Kentucky, right down the hill and into the recently gentrified shopping district with its genuine cobblestone streets.

I leapt upon his tumbling body with both feet. Goliath Brigadoon, in his helpless, prone, and accelerating fall, had put me in mind of a sturdy log, and I proceeded to ride him past the lively storefronts like a lumberjack in the act of logrolling, much to the delight of the tourists emerging from the taffy shops and calendar stores on the one side of the street that was not leveled in the course of our journey.

Look at him go, I recognized as the content of their unspo-ken delight. That man can surely put on a show. Surely this is the greatest form of entertainment we have ever seen.

Goliath Brigadoon came to rest at the foot of a quaint gazebo where the mayor was engaged in making a speech. The crowd erupted in cheers.

Why goodness gracious who are you, said the mayor. Surely you've come to assassinate me.

Nothing could be further from the truth, I assured him. May I inquire as to the subject of your current speech?

As you can see this is the day when everyone dresses his cat or dog in a little costume and we have a parade, said the mayor.

Looking out at the crowd, I could see that the mayor was telling the truth. Every person there held a small cat or dog dressed as Robin Hood, Zorro, a chef, or some other fanciful character.

May I inquire as to the purpose of this display? I asked.

You may, replied the mayor. It's to drum up business.

Something was amiss. I decided to give the populace a lec-ture on pet rearing.

What are you people doing to your pets may I ask. Some-thing obscene. My downstairs neighbor and formerly betrothed, Glorious Jones, was often seen to make out with her cat, the whimsically monickered General Stonewall Pussy. I'm not implying anything too grotesque, just some delicate tongue-kissing, the very tips of the tongues and nothing more, a mere show of affection, nothing to be alarmed about, you all should try it. Certainly it would be preferable to the pathos before me. I want to see all of you tonguing your pets, nothing too rough, and forget about all this dressing them up in costumes business, which robs them of their dignity.

Thus inspired, the mob indulged in a communal orgy of pet kissing, mere pecks and the slightest hint of tongue, nothing too gross at all.

That dude knows everything. This is the best time I've had in my life. Hats off to that incredible dude. These were a few of their apparent thoughts.

Well sir, that's all very fine and dandy, said the mayor, but what are we going to do for Pets on Parade Day now? Everyone will stay concealed in their homes, making out with their pets, and there will be nothing for the tourists to get worked up about.

Listen up, folks, I said. I'm going to invent a sport right now. It's the annual festivity for which your town will soon be known. I call it naked human logrolling. The unconscious human who acts as the log, such as your friend and neighbor Goliath Brigadoon here, will remain fully clothed. The roller, such as myself, however, shall strip down to nothing, like so.

With that, I tore off my garments, hopped on top of Goliath Brigadoon's supine figure with both feet, and rolled him down the hill, down the pier, which crashed beneath our combined weight, and into the sparkling lake from which the town got its name, the townspeople wondering at the perfection of my large, muscular, and entirely hairless buttocks, which glowed from within as if fashioned from costliest alabaster.

The motion of my feet was so fast that Goliath Brigadoon did not sink, but acted rather as a kind of paddle wheeler. I floated him out to an island in the middle of the lake, from which I observed the tiny people at the end of the broken pier like ants marveling at me from afar. My member dangled across the shore and the head of it dipped into the water. I stood with my hands on my hips, beaming with satisfaction.

Night came to the little island.

Goliath Brigadoon slowly awakened from the slumber into which I had pummeled him. You may be sure that his senses were rewarded by the odor of a delicious repast. I had scoured the island for all the turtle eggs and duck eggs I could find, and fried them up, shells and all, in a satellite dish that had washed up on shore. I had then slaughtered all the turtles and ducks on the island, making a large turtle soup and cooking the ducks slowly, in their own fat, by the French method, both of the latter dishes prepared in large chemical drums.

What smells so good? asked Goliath Brigadoon.

His groggy manner and slurred speech indicated that his return to consciousness was incomplete, so I buggered him back to reality, achieving thunderous climax six times over the course of four hours.

My heart wasn't in it, but Goliath Brigadoon declared it to be the first sexual contact he had enjoyed with another man that he knew of, and pronounced it delightful. I showed my gratitude by bringing him to climax twice, not through physical contact, but by standing on the other side of the island and humming at a certain frequency that only whales can hear. It was the least I could do. I knew I was overcompensating for my lack of real feeling.

After dinner Goliath Brigadoon and I lay on the sand, nude and gigantic, picking our teeth and smoking corncob pipes in a companionable stupor, my head at rest on his commodious and extremely furry belly.

Say Goliath, I drawled amidst the creaking and tooting of the night animals and the crackling of the cozy fire. You were going to tell me all about hay.

I'm afeared that if'n I tells you all bout hay, you'll be nigh bout done with me, and I wawnt never see you never again no more, came his touching reply. I jes dawnt know hows my pore ole brain could go bout handlin such a tragidity.

I won't lie to you, Goliath Brigadoon. I'm a wandering man. I go about like the wind. It's what I do. Can you understand that in your simple country way? Can you understand a man like me, Goliath Brigadoon?

Good gorphin gopher bones, exclaimed Goliath Brigadoon. I jes kint swoggle hown no minfoke never knowed whut der deedle durn duddle dink daw doogle dumpin jar jar doo doodle nug ner never did nurk der dern divvied down duggle dog dump.

There, there, I replied. I sat up so I could cradle his big sobbing head in my lap.

23

Here are the findings on hay that I coaxed out of Goliath Brigadoon:

Haystacks are largely a thing of the past. It would follow that needles in haystacks, already rare when haystacks were in general usage, have dwindled to virtual extinction.

What accounts for the rarity of haystacks?

The dome-topped haystacks of yore were designed to shed water as efficiently as possible as the hay stood out in the open fields. The very tops and bottoms tended to get wet, but the middle portions remained marvelously protected. With the advent of the nineteenth century's horse-drawn baling machines, however, baling—as opposed to stacking—became the preferred method, and actual stacks of hay were suddenly obsolete. It's simple economics: if you can't afford a baling machine, you must stack your hay, but if you can't afford to bale it, chances are you're not making hay to begin with.

In answer to my final question of practicality, how high must hay be stacked before I might legitimately call it a haystack, Goliath Brigadoon replied that any particular farmer who, for whatever odd reason, was still stacking hay, when baling was so much more sensible and convenient, would tend to stack his hay as high as he could pitch it, in the neighborhood of twelve feet in the air.

I left poor Goliath howling for my favors on the island. I made, over my shoulder, empty promises of an imminent return, though I knew in my heart I would never see him again. It was best for both of us, but the truth would have taken too long to explain to his poor, sweet brain. If only I could have said to him, Look, Goliath Brigadoon, I beat you up out of frustration and buggered you to mask the pangs of thwarted love, and used you for your hay information. Oh, but what cruelty it would have been to tell him that, to watch his uncomprehending eyes, his gaping mouth emitting its seemingly infinite stores of saliva.

I swam to shore as the town slept and peeked through the third-floor window of the local library, where I spied an antique globe.

Where? Where to find old-fashioned haystacks? I dismissed

the Pennsylvania Amish country out of hand, for surely they used the horse-drawn balers that Goliath had described. Who, then, would worry so about horses as to excuse them from harsh labor? Of course. Hippies. And where was the best place to find hippies? California.

I smashed the window with the tip of my finger, intending to pull the globe closer for a more detailed look. The noise awoke a prudish young librarian who had fallen asleep at her desk and been accidentally locked in the building.

Her name was Maisie. She wore chunky black-rimmed glasses in the cat-eye mold, a severe bun of hair, a dowdy expression, and clothing which did not flatter her figure.

You're wet, she observed with a librarian's scowl. Wetness leads to foxing and other diseases of paper.

It was then that she had the misfortune of gazing into my eyes.

I've often wondered what it must be like for another person to gaze into my eyes. I've gazed into my own eyes, of course, with the aid of a mirror, and yes, I've felt some inkling of a swoon, some ineffable lostness. I might say without exaggeration that many times I've fallen into the double double-mirror of my chocolaty pupils (me looking at me in me looking at me in me looking at me forever and ever) couched in their sky-irises, fallen, yes, in love.

Oh God, I want to desecrate literature with you, said Maisie the librarian.

Good Lord. Was I nothing more than a happy giant who loved to eat and copulate? Yes, I could easily imagine dear Maisie shaking her head back and forth until her bun of hair was loosed and sprawled about her head in a wanton array, imagine her removing her glasses, tearing at her garments to show the quaint but ravishing architecture of garters, belts, and pulleys beneath, the shape of her gossamer-coated calves, her bare pink thighs.

But what if I could not give this deserving librarian the gratification she craved? In my brain, which had produced every possible type of thought over the years, I had never considered such a thing. Perhaps my brain was running out of new types of things to think, and had thus begun to explore its few remaining options. Or perhaps my misunderstanding with Glorious Jones had nudged me toward self-doubt.

If justified, self-doubt may have a salubrious effect on the doubter, may teach him, in the end, how great he truly is, if only for recognizing the warning signals of some particular spiritual corruption and thus avoiding it in a manly fashion. In these ideal conditions, self-doubt is, actually, self-affirmation.

On the other hand, unjustified self-doubt may be recognized by its exact similitude to justified self-doubt. In fact, the more justified the self-doubt seems, the more likely it is, in reality, its own counterfeit.

Listen, I said to Maisie the saucy librarian. I have mixed feelings about what should happen next. True self-doubt is self-affirmation. False self-doubt is self-doubt. But if self-doubt is self-affirmation, wouldn't that make false self-doubt, which is real self-doubt, self-affirmation? And in that case, isn't everything self-affirmation?

You're blowing my mind with your intellectualism, said Maisie. You're turning me on so bad. I'm so hot. I'm going to do a wrong thing. I can't hold it in. I'm going to pee all over the collected works of Harold Pinter.

And I was like, It's a free country, baby.

But watching was an empty experience.

25

I made my way to California, using my extraordinary sense of smell to seek out the largest possible concentrations of patchouli and vanilla extract, the two favored perfumes of female hippies. Foot odor is common to hippies both male and female. Were I to list all odors associated with hippies there would be room for little else. Hippies are not as monolithic as one might think, aromatically speaking. There are subtleties I can't go into here. I'll say that stereotypes are by and large inaccurate, and leave it at that.

I had moral qualms, smelling people without their knowledge. A person's smells are more private than his thoughts.

26

I found myself near Stockton, California, in a field of majestic haystacks as far as the eye could see. But where were the hippies?

I knew of Stockton's reputation as a peaceful backwater devoid of troublemakers—indeed the scene before me confirmed that picture—but this was where I had been led by my own infallible nose.

Just when I had begun to question my accuracy of smell—and therefore everything that presented, or seemed to present, itself to my senses—the hippies burst out from secret passageways hidden inside or beneath the haystacks, swarmed forth from what I could only assume was a complex system of underground burrows, scores of hippies, nude hippies, ululating in a fearsome manner. Smeared with mud and fecal matter, brandishing staffs formed of woven hay, teeth unbrushed and coifs replete with lice and tangles, their young breasts flapping hither and yon, their dingdongs flipping round and about, their vaccination marks in full view, their excessive pubic hair waving crab-filled in the soft summer's breeze, they approached and circled me with their terrifying yodels, terrifying, that is, to the type of man likely to be terrified, which I was not. If anything, I found the scene to hold a certain wry charm as the sun set slowly in the west.

Good for you, I shouted. Well done, well done. I see what

you're going for here. A return to Stonehenge, an homage to Easter Island, or wait, the Dionysian mysteries, out here catching baby rabbits no doubt, hell on hay, biting their heads off, tearing them apart like the bacchants of Euripides, yes, quite bracing, very entertaining, marvelous fun for the whole family. I have a feeling we're all going to be great friends.

The crowd of hippies parted, and a little man hobbled toward me, a man no more than four feet eleven inches tall, with furry leggings intended to remind one of goat legs, shiny leather shoes intended to remind one of goat hooves, little nubbins of horns rubber-cemented to his forehead, and a hairy little chest. The aureoles surrounding his nipples were disproportionately large, and of an unusual violet hue. In so many ways this curious fellow made me think of a smaller Goliath Brigadoon. He was compact and comely. The hippies grew silent, according him respect.

Hello, my name is Stan, he said.

Hello.

We've prayed for your arrival and here you are.

That's irrational.

Exactly, he said. Did you know that Stanford University was founded upon the advice of a ghost? It's a fact easily checkable in books. Leland Stanford's dead son asked him the favor, and he complied. Cal Tech was founded by Jack Parsons, a disciple of the black magician Aleister Crowley. Look it up anywhere.

Only in California, I said.

Yes, those two examples are from California, said Stan. But what if I told you that Maureen Reagan saw Lincoln's ghost in the White House? You might object that Ronald Reagan was the former governor of California. But Lincoln himself, who hailed from Kentucky and Illinois, once observed two prophetic faces looking back at him from the mirror, one sickly and wan, representing his assassination in his second term. Hart Crane gazed through the window of the subway car and saw Edgar Allan Poe reflected there. In 1677, several Puritan women tore apart some Indians in the kind of Dionysian fury you've just been kind enough to mention. On May 19, 1780, the sun didn't shine in New England. Verifiable by any almanac. Many of the founding fathers belonged to the secret society of Masons. The role of spiritualism in abolition and women's suffrage: would those movements have occurred otherwise? We could cross our fingers, but that would be irrational. Theosophy. Blavatsky. Mesmerism. Malcom X. For this and many other reasons we're going to cut your wiener off.

That's completely irrational, I said.

Exactly, said Stan. From his leggings he retrieved a scimitar and wielded it with expertise.

Hold on just a minute, I said. You seem like an interesting

kind of guy, Stan, and I'd like to discuss your ideas more fully.

There'll be plenty of time for that after I cut off your wiener, said Stan. Lie down.

I did as he asked, to show that I meant no harm. A couple of his friends gave Stan a boost and he made his way up my leg toward my lap.

Swoop, swoop, swoop, went the knife, each swoop coming closer to the crotch of my pants.

Is it your intention to ruin my pants as well? I asked.

Your pants may be removed if you wish.

I had dressed for the occasion in the garments of a Native American Indian, including an elaborate headdress, thus to impress whatever hippies I happened to run across.

Stan stopped swooping the knife and rested in my commodious and welcoming navel as I scooted out of my impressively fringed buffalo-hide pants. A regiment of hippies came forward, folded them neatly, and put them away.

There it is, said Stan. Oh boy, this is going to take a lot of swooping.

There is an option we have for the faint of heart, said Stan.

I'm all ears, I said. Although I was not faint of heart, I wanted to explore all my options.

We can feed you magical mushrooms until you go into a

stupor. Then you don't feel it as much when your wiener comes flying off.

See, now I think I'm getting to the root of your troubles, I said. All this talk of mysticism and such. The mushroom's effect on the human brain can be explained quite rationally through the process of chemistry. But sure, I'll try some, just to see what all the fuss is about.

By this time the sun had gone down and the haystacks loomed eerily in the gathering dusk. A funnel was inserted into my mouth and mushrooms were packed into my gullet by means of a kind of ceremonial mortar operated by two lovely young nude female cultists. After about ten minutes, several gallons of mushrooms had entered my system.

How's it going? said Stan.

Dandy like candy, I replied.

More mushrooms were shoved into my gullet. This went on for some time.

Surely you're feeling a little something by now, said Stan.

More mushrooms, I said.

The night was dark and two or three haystacks had been made into bonfires for the illumination of the ritual.

Well, this is the most mushrooms anyone has ever eaten. Are you sure nothing's happening?

I'm as cool as a cucumber, I said.

Stan requested another basket of the mushrooms.

Toward dawn one of Stan's followers worked up the nerve to question him.

Check this cat out, said the scrawny young man. He's ate up like all our shrooms. He must be like a visitor from the stars or whatever. Nothing fazes this cat. Let's just cut his wanger off already.

That's not according to the law, said Stan. He's not stultified.

Far from it, I said.

But we're out of shrooms, said the scrawny acolyte.

Borrow some, said Stan.

The empiricists have some, but they're our sworn enemy, said Scrawny.

The law is the law, said Stan.

I don't know who the devil these empiricists are, but what about this? I said. What if I go to their encampment and steal enough mushrooms to restore your supplies? And then if I eat six more bushels with no noticeable effect, you can cut my wiener off no matter what.

That sounds like a fair deal, said Stan.

We shook on it.

Dawn rose over the haystacks. Lovely nude women between the ages of eighteen and twenty-four gave me a ritual bath and dressed me in the shamanistic garb of a human haystack. Or at least that was the plan. When they calculated the amount of hay it would take to disguise me properly, they opted instead to nestle a single haystack betwixt my pectorals in a symbolic nod to chest hair, with which, in my smoothness and bareness, I had not been blessed.

There wouldn't happen to be a needle in there, I said.

Ha ha, they said.

Ha ha ha, I said.

30

Scrawny and I went through the hayfield and into the bordering forest, toward the lair of the empiricists. To better escape detection, I wallowed on my belly, thinking how awesome it was that I was making a path for whoever wanted to walk through the woods at a later date. Maybe one day a paved road would be built over whatever I had flattened. I was the living embodiment of progress and enlightenment. Scrawny hung on to a couple of my neck hairs and enjoyed pretending they were reins.

This is a good time to rob them, man, in the broad daylight. They sleep by day and gather their mushrooms by the light of the moon, said Scrawny. He was dressed as a haystack, but in his scrawniness did not much resemble one. Also, his hay was sparse and looked kind of thrown together at the last minute. The dark green makeup smeared under his eyes, however, was effective in a cheap way.

Will anyone be guarding the mushrooms? I asked.

Oh sure. But I'll grab him from behind and slit his throat with my little straight razor.

Is that necessary? I asked.

We hippies are a gentle lot until you get us riled. You watch yourself when we get close. You don't know these empiricists. They've got some crazy strong mojo going out there in the woods. They're probably all keyed up and frenzied from their magic ceremonies. That's the screwy thing about these empiricists, man. They've got over two thousand pages of witchcraft spells from Tudor and Stuart England, and they're trying out every one of them, just to prove they don't work. Some hate it so much they get addicted, man. Those are the cats you got to watch out for.

You know, Scrawny, I'm enamored of your use of the word cat as a living relic of slang terminology. I'm going to have to remember to pepper my speech patterns with it, for accessibility. Lately I've been using dude and freaky a lot, with excellent results.

Yeah, you should stick with those, said Scrawny. Those are good. Cat is my thing.

One cannot own a word, Scrawny. Information wants to be free.

You can't get inside my head, man, not with all the Geiger counters in the world.

Fair enough. In the words of Matthew Arnold, A God, a

God their severance ruled! / And bade betwixt their shores to be
/ The unplumb'd, salt, estranging sea.

This Matthew Arnold sounds like one uptight cat. You can't
pull me into your dead world of smartness.

We presently discerned that we were nearing the site of the
mushrooms, for we happened upon two idle and complacent
guards. Scrawny and I eavesdropped.

You know, said the one, I believe I have the most complete
private library in existence of works on the subject of corn.

I wish you wouldn't talk about it all the time, said the
other.

I've made a few recent acquisitions which may surprise you,
said the first guard. A full set, bound in kidskin, of the British
Corn Laws, up to and including the modifications of 1815.

I'm going to start a blog, said the second guard.

And what will be the subject of your blog? inquired the first.

How I go around getting rowdy with my chums, and all the
scrapes we get into on account of drinking schnapps.

Ah, but you don't have any chums.

I plan to get some. I'm going to call them "mates," like they
do in England.

I know what you should make a blog about, said the first
guard. All the times you've been fired.

It's a thought, said the second. No, that's good.

Remember when you got fired for sitting around with no

shoes on while the guy was trying to fix your computer? And your feet were in his face.

I was wearing athletic socks.

Dirty athletic socks. And you were eating a big pickle for lunch and it made everybody sick.

Yes, I remember.

How about the time you were walking around the candy store with your shirt off?

But the second guard did not get a chance to defend himself, for Scrawny had decapitated him.

The guard's head lay on the ground, expressing confusion.

Before the first guard could raise his shepherd's crook in defense, Scrawny had decapitated him as well.

Oh, look at you, said the first guard's head. You're a mess.

How can our heads still be talking? said the second. We need to amass data.

The first guard tried to reply, but his mouth just made an airy noise like cha cha cha cha cha and his eyes rolled back and forth.

The second guard began doing the same as the first guard.

Cha cha cha cha cha cha cha cha.

Cha cha cha cha cha cha cha cha cha.

Cha cha cha cha.

Cha cha cha.

It was an eerie sight.

3/

We made it back to the fields of hay. I was on all fours, dragging six hundred pounds of psychedelic mushrooms in a large net, pulling it by means of a bit between my teeth. Scrawny rode on the back of my neck, whooping with delight and gaily waving his bloody straight razor in the sparkling air.

The hippies had dressed in tattered high school band uniforms, and greeted our arrival with a clamorous honking on various rusted and broken instruments. Their ruckus was harsh but sweet, touching in its boundless ineptitude. This, I believe, is what the kids mean by irony, and the death of irony, and my knowing tears rained freely on the dry fields, and wherever my teardrops fell, flowers grew—rare African orchids, unknown in this clime. This is scientifically explainable by the fact of some spores that I probably got in my eye one time without knowing it.

Stan came forth.

Good news, pal, he said to me, and really to all assembled. We have decided not to cut off your wiener.

Huzzah, huzzah, said the hippies. Perhaps little Scrawny was the happiest of all.

You have brought us the sacred mushroom, and for that we honor you. You must perform a certain task, however. I'm sorry, but that is the law. All you have to do is find the needle that we have hidden in the haystack you see before you, our mightiest haystack, fifteen feet in height.

You call that a haystack? I said. Fifteen feet is nothing to me, no offense. I won't feel right about this whole thing until you push together all your haystacks, forming one haystack of great and mammoth enormity, with just one little needle inside. That's the only way I can see this being satisfying for any of us.

You've got a point, said Stan. The next day he began overseeing construction of the world's largest haystack, a process that took a number of months to complete. In the meantime I squatted on my haunches and thought about stuff. Several forest animals and some hippies took refuge from bad weather in the steady, unmoving shadow of my thoughtful haunches.

When one morning I saw that the haystack had been completed, and stood some 150 feet in height, I rejected the golden scimitar of Stan in favor of the less ceremonial but more practical tin roof that had blown off a shed in a storm, and with it leapt to the top of the haystack, in order to address the crowd and reveal my astonishing true purpose.

My word is my bond, I said. In a single inimitable gesture, I brought down my rustic makeshift guillotine of sharp-edged tin and sliced off my own wiener. It rolled down the haystack and into the midst of the startled hippies, crushing to death three of them who were too slow to get out of the way, including, sadly, Scrawny. Out of deep respect and in solemn remembrance, I crossed out cat from my vocabulary.

Why? cried the hippies.

Let me put it in regular language that anyone can understand, I replied. I'm sure you remember the story about some old Zen dude that was pointing all the time, and this second dude was always wondering what the heck that was all about, and finally he asked him, Hey, how come you're pointing all the time, and the old Zen dude cut off this other dude's finger and then the second dude was like, Oh yeah, I totally get what Zen is all about. That's kind of the feeling I got when I cut off my own wiener. Liberating, I guess you'd call it. Like, hey, I've been relying too much on my wiener. Like, wow, this isn't as bad as I thought. Like, maybe I can learn a little something from cutting off my own wiener.

A van screeched up. Its markings indicated that it was from the Center for Disease Control in Atlanta, Georgia. Four big men in white scrambled out and wrestled my detached wiener into submission. It put up an amazing fight, like a tuna on the deck of a tuna boat in a movie of Italian neorealism. Somebody shot it with a tranquilizer gun, then the guys got together and loaded it into the back of the van. They roared off as quickly as they had come. Some hippies were employed the whole time in climbing the haystack to pat down my hurt place with a poultice of soothing herbs and bind it with a special bandage woven from hay, so I could do very little about the abduction. What little satisfaction I got came from calling out zingers to the retreating van, such as, Hey, where's my receipt? and Be careful with that, boys, I'm kind of attached to it.

32

How would cutting off my own wiener affect my love life?

Not very much, I assumed.

Love isn't just about hanky panky.

Plus, what good had my giant wiener ever done me? I wasn't in love with a giant woman. I was in love with Glorious Jones.

33

I lay down on my back in the field so that Stan's yurt—which was believed by the hippies to have mysterious curative qualities— could be relocated over my wound. Stan sat in the open flap of the yurt, which faced my upper body, and gazed upon me with respect and admiration.

Wow, buddy, was all that Stan could say.

It's not so bad, I said, lifting my head a bit to give him a wink.

I can't believe it, said Stan. Here you are with your wiener cut off and you're the one reassuring me.

Stan, you're a special person, I said. This is some kind of organization you've put together. Your hippies seem to respect you a lot. And that's an accomplishment you can be proud of. I don't want you to ever, ever forget it. All this negative talk about who's reassuring whom will never get us anywhere.

I can't believe your amount of wisdom, said Stan.

I know you can't, I said, and that's perfectly okay. You need to be okay with that.

Okay, said Stan.

There's the old Stan, I said. Listen, Stan, you could do me a favor that would be a big help to me.

Name it.

It's an idea that came to me while I was cutting off my wiener. Now, you might not know this, but I came here on purpose to look for a needle in a haystack.

That's wild, said Stan. And we just hid a needle in a haystack for you, as part of your redemptive ritual. Remember? And then you got up there and cut your wiener off instead. Wow.

Stan shook his head and I could only guess at his many emotions.

See how things work out? I said. Awesomely is how most things work out. When will people ever learn to admit it? They're all too hung up on making their own problems.

Wait, wait, said Stan. He was jotting down my aphorisms in a little book.

The wisdom of the ages, I said self-deprecatingly. No, now listen. I've been worried about the actual logistics of finding a needle in a haystack, but in the split second I was cutting off my own wiener the solution came to me. If I take the needle out of the haystack, it will no longer be a needle in a haystack. It will be a needle formerly in a haystack, or a needle *from*, not *in*, a haystack, and I will have failed. What I need is the whole needle-bearing haystack—a needleinahaystack, if you get my meaning. Imagine needle-in-a-haystack as a single word, a single concept. If I had been asked to find a ship in a bottle, for example, I wouldn't be asked to remove the ship from the bottle, would I? I'm reminded of an old vaudeville joke, which I can't quite remember. I believe a fellow was injured by tomatoes. The joke was they were still in the can. I'm not telling it right. You'll find it elucidated in Thurber, I believe. What I mean to say is, without the haystack surrounding it, the needle would just be a needle. What I request of you, Stan, is the entire haystack. Will you give me that haystack?

With my greatest blessings, said Stan.

After a period of convalescence I was brought to the haystack with the needle in it, which I carried on my back to the outskirts of town. The hippies had followed me part of the way, their eyes full of tears, but now I was alone.

As I stood there at the crossroads with my bundle on my back, the 150-foot haystack large and burdensome even to me, my image resonated profoundly on many levels. I'm sure that any passing scholar would have had a field day with me, while the common folk would have been struck by feelings they could not name, feelings of connection with something universal.

I was Atlas, I suppose, with my famous burden, or, to the etymological community, the semblance of an ant writ large.

I was John Bunyan's Christian at the outset of his journey.

I turned these thoughts and emblems over and over in my head like precious jewels with many facets until it occurred to me that while my mind had been focused on these things of a higher nature, I also should have been paying attention to my physical surroundings. I had walked all the way to Pennsylvania, where the terrain had become quite rough, and I had stumbled now and again. What if the needle had dropped out of the haystack somewhere along the way?

Just to be sure, I stopped, took the haystack apart, found the needle, and put the haystack back together, leaving the needle precisely where I had found it.

Was it now the same haystack? True, my unparalleled mind, with its perfect memory, had helped me put the stack back together in the exact way it had been before, straw for straw. But did that make it the same haystack, or was I taking shortcuts and playing loose and fast with the rules?

Problems like this would only increase as I found more objects and carried them around for safekeeping.

My hunt would take me, perchance, all over the world—mayhap, the cosmos. It would be counterproductive to worry all the time. I needed a mobile storage unit that I could pull behind me wherever I went.

And so from the ground I forged myself a mighty wagon.

Plunging my arms elbow deep in the iron-rich earth I brought forth the necessary ore. Raising my body temperature to the appropriate levels through intense self-determination, I was able to produce enough of the raw material necessary for my purpose. As an unexpected side effect, the soil all around my superheated body was transformed into colored glass of rarest beauty, which, as I understand it, was later broken into attractive pieces and sold by the grateful community of the area, who, until my appearance, had toiled in relative poverty.

But none of that concerned me at the moment. My one goal, which I accomplished with astounding rapidity, was to fashion a giant iron wagon in which to carry the various objects of my quest.

And the wheels were made from pieces of a mountain.

I hid my wagon—the haystack resting in its bed—in a condemned parking garage, and took a trip to Egypt, where I gathered sufficient roots of the madder plant to squeeze out a bedazzling dye—rose madder by name—with which to coat my wagon in red, that beloved and traditional hue.

I found that I had underestimated the girth of my wagon.

Rather than make another trip to Egypt, I opened one of my veins and painted the neglected spots with the blood of my body.

When the wagon was thus painted, I held up the bottom floor of the abandoned parking garage on my shoulders, and smashed its concrete buttresses into a fine white powder, which I mixed with the saliva of my mouth and the sweat of my own feet to produce a subtle white pigmentation. And with this white I did name my wagon, and inscribe the name thereon in the elegant cursive of my long-admired penmanship. And I called my wagon Ol' Tuffy.

After that I was tired, so I checked into a nice bed-and-breakfast in a historic part of the dairy farming region of Vermont. I could not fit into the main house, of course, but room was cleared out for me in the barn, which had been converted into a rather homey factory for the making of artisanal cheese. It was a slow time in the cheese-making process, when the cheese itself was doing most of the work, so I would be afforded a modicum of privacy. In the natural light there, amid the inaudible burble of slowly ripening curd and the kindly lowing and reassuring musk of the cattle in the pasture nearby, I opened the second envelope and read what Glorious Jones had written:

DE SOTO'S BONES

So that was the way she wanted to play it. Touché, Glorious

Jones, I congratulated her within the secret parts of my skull. Your night classes in history really paid off.

As she had probably considered de Soto's bones impossible to find, I felt no compunction about employing a countermove that equaled hers in deviousness. I placed a telephone call to a service representative employed on behalf of my American Express black card, or the black AmEx as it is abbreviated by people who have one. The service is what sets it apart. A friend of mine saw a horse he liked in a movie, and the black card representatives found it in Europe—that actual, individual horse out of all the horses in the world—and negotiated the sale and subsequent delivery with impressive speediness.

Hello, this is Sally, how may I help you today?

My goodness, Sally. Has anyone ever told you you have the rapturous voice of a legendary siren?

Yes sir. The last gentleman it was my pleasure to serve told me just that, thank you. I must say it is a pleasantry that never gets old, if I may be allowed to be so bold, with your permission, of course.

I would ask for nothing less from a black card service representative, Sally. Maybe you've run across some people in your life who think boldness is unattractive in a woman. Why, my thinking is just the opposite. I admire that you have what it takes to make it in this business world of today.

I'm gratified, sir.

And I'm gratified that you're gratified. You know, Sally, talking to you is like talking to a lifelong friend. I'm sure we could chat all day. Perhaps one day we'll meet face-to-face and do just that. In the meantime, however, it is your professional skills, rather than your exemplary personality, which is of the most pressing urgency to me.

Of course, sir. Please go on.

Well, Sally, by the way, that's a beautiful name, it's my favorite name, actually, Sally. Sally, what I need from you is de Soto's bones.

I'll be glad to acquire the item or items you need, sir. I'm afraid I'm unclear, just at the moment, as to what it is, or what they are. Bones, did you say? Forgive me for asking you to repeat yourself. Here at American Express Black we pride ourselves on a certain immediacy, which I fear I have let lapse in this present instance.

You're too hard on yourself, Sally. Now there's no need on earth that you should know right off the bat what I mean by de Soto's bones.

Thank you for saying so, sir. Your call is being recorded for quality assurance.

Well, I couldn't be more pleased. And I think that anyone listening in to this call will be forced to admit that you have demonstrated an extraordinary range of skills in dealing with a most extraordinary request.

And an extraordinary man, if I may be allowed to say so, sir.

Your voice is like honey, Sally, sweet honey straight from the comb.

I would like to mention a particular story from the Old Testament at this juncture, sir, if that would give no offense.

No, Sally, of course not. I believe the Bible to be a fascinating piece of literature.

I have Jesus in my heart, sir.

I fully support your right to believe as you wish, Sally.

May I be so bold as to quote directly from the Bible, sir?

You may.

It's against company policy, sir. I don't know why I feel compelled. It could cost me my job.

Sally, when people talk to me, they are moved to do things they can't explain. It's the nature of my charisma. And were you to lose your job over such a trifling matter, well, American Express would lose, in turn, one of its very best customers.

Sally sobbed at my largesse.

You were going to quote from the Bible, I said to cheer her up.

"And he turned aside to see the carcass of the lion: and, behold, there was a swarm of bees and honey in the carcass of the lion."

Now what on earth made you think of that, Sally?

Something you said reminded me of it, sir. It's one of the twelve great deeds of Samson, how he killed a lion with his bare hands. I hope it isn't amiss for me to say so.

Of course not, Sally, of course not, my dear.

Might I read from another section of the Old Testament, sir?

Why, I wouldn't miss it. May I suggest, Sally, that if you do lose your job—and it's certainly not a circumstance I foresee— you could make something of a name for yourself reading parts of the Bible out loud to piano accompaniment in cabarets as part of a one-woman show. You could win a Tony, Sally, and I'm not just saying that to be polite.

"My beloved put in his hand by the hole of the door, and my bowels were moved for him. I rose up to open to my beloved; and my hands dropped with myrrh, and my fingers with sweet smelling myrrh, upon the handles of the lock."

Goodness, that's some hot stuff.

I'm afraid for my soul, sir. I'm afraid that if I ever met you in person I would surrender my virginity too willingly.

Well, Sally, we'll cross that bridge when we come to it.

I think you know what they mean by the hole of the door, sir.

Yes, Sally, I think I do.

And bowels, sir.

Yes, of course, and bowels.

I know what's going to happen now, sir. You're going to request a different service representative because of my unprofessional behavior.

Sally, dear Sally, calm yourself, I beg of you. I'm going to tell you a secret that will help you feel better. I'm a man without a member, Sally.

A man without a member, sir?

A wiener, Sally. I have no wiener, to be specific. Plus, I'm betrothed to another, if only she'll have me back. We giggle a lot and kiss each other against the stove and it's very serious.

Sally, let me lay it on you in an easygoing, colloquial way that will allow you to absorb large concepts. Hernando de Soto was the dude that wanted to take over Florida. Everybody was like, Dude, this isn't even Florida anymore and you're still taking stuff over, and he was like, Florida is whatever I say it is, so back off. In a way, I guess you could say he was my kind of guy. But in another way he was a bad dude who I think hurt a lot of people and didn't even cry about it. So around 1541 he made it to the western bank of the Mississippi River and everybody was saying, Where's all the gold you promised us? And Hernando de Soto was all, I know it's around here somewhere. Keep looking. I can identify with his optimism. In a way, I too am searching for gold, but it's spiritual gold. Maybe Hernando de Soto should have looked for spiritual gold instead of regular gold, and then he'd still be around and me and him would be having some laughs and kicking it old school. But what happened was he died. He died on the banks of the Mississippi, and some buddies of his buried him right there in the water. Nobody knows the exact location.

If I had had a teacher like you I would never have dropped out of school, said Sally.

She fiddled with her computer for a couple of minutes and said that American Express could locate and transport de Soto's bones, no problem. It might take as long as three months, though, and she was worried that the delay would upset me.

I told her that three months sounded perfect. She was blown away.

Now all I had to do was sit back and wait for de Soto's bones. I asked the proprietress of the bed-and-breakfast to hold all my calls for three months. I was beginning to lay the ground-work for hibernation.

According to the rules as put forth by lawyer Hap Martin, I was not allowed to begin hunting the third item before the second one was found. With nothing on my agenda, there was no bet-ter time for a long, refreshing hibernation to get me ready for the remainder of my quest.

I placed a call to my robot ward, Jimmy, and ordered him to drive up and put in place a system of laser beams that would guarantee my complete security, afterward affixing the Do Not Disturb sign to the barn door by means of a powerful epoxy that would never weaken or dissolve.

He came right away and began attending to my needs.

When will you be coming home, master? asked Jimmy upon the completion of his task. I'm so terribly lonely there.

Why, that's impossible, Jimmy. You haven't been endowed with the proper circuitry.

To pine away in solitude, to wish one could die. Is this what it means to be…human? said Jimmy.

You've been watching too much television, Jimmy. You're parroting the inaccurately portrayed complaints of countless fictional robots. How many angry letters have I written to *Entertainment Weekly* on this very subject? Let me put it to you this way. With that, I poked a screwdriver into Jimmy's computer brain, disabling his perambulatory nodules.

Why, master, why? said Jimmy. If you make my legs work again, we can go bowling.

I gave a good, solid twist to his vocalization center, dislocating it.

Agghhhkkkk, said Jimmy. Zzzzzgurrrrrzzzk.

This is for your own good, Jimmy, I said. If you were experiencing—or believed yourself to be experiencing—positive so-called emotions, such as peppiness, I would be inclined to let you be. Even that would be wrong, though my good nature would undoubtedly make allowances. But whining is unbecoming in any creature, and mechanistically reproduced whining is something very close to an abomination.

I reduced Jimmy to his basic elements and hid him in an antique butter churn.

I ate three hundred bunches of green bananas, two hundred bushel baskets of beefsteak tomatoes, ten bags of jumbo marshmallows, eight trays of Italian wedding cookies, eight boxes of frozen vegetarian sausage patties, sixty-two barbecue chicken burritos, eight Chinese takeaway cartons of steamed pot stickers, a dozen mason jars of pickled watermelon rind, four bottles of ketchup, six heads of red cabbage, eighteen boxes of chocolate-covered cherries, eight crates of fresh blueberries, a box of Fruity Pebbles, ten whole pineapples, four hundred loaves of crusty French bread, twenty-seven buckets of fresh-shucked Pismo clams, a ramekin of squash casserole, ten dozen Butterfinger candy bars, a gross of Krystal hamburgers, twelve hundred Krispy Kreme plain cake doughnuts, a thousand Oreos, a twelve-ounce chunk of the highest quality Parmesan cheese, forty pork chops pan fried in garlic butter with white wine and orange juice, forty baked pork chops stuffed with chestnuts and sage, fourteen Concord grapes, thirty-three broiled softshell crabs, two hundred gallons of béchamel sauce, six hundred new potatoes boiled in milk, sixty gallons of mulligan stew, sixty gallons of Brunswick stew (hold the beans), sixty gallons of bouillabaisse, sixty gallons of borscht, sixty-four gallons of matzo ball soup, sixty-four gallons of Jell-O brand butterscotch pudding, eighty rashers of bacon, twelve links of raw Italian sausage (spicy), ten links of mild, eighty biscuits floating in a twenty-five gallon cauldron of hot, peppery flour gravy, one hundred bunches of flat Italian parsley, six bunches of flavorless curly parsley, nine dozen raw oysters, a traditional Denver omelet, forty pots of black coffee laced with cardamom and ammonia, and enough piping hot apple fritters to fill thirteen wheelbarrows.

I topped everything off with nature's sleep aid: eighty-eight gallons of warm milk with a dash of nutmeg.

Now I was ready.

I lay down with the aging cheeses, contemplating them moist and restful in their rinds. How like a cheese I was.

Using extraordinary concentration and exercising my sphincter in a particular manner, I managed to squeeze out several yards of a delicately attractive yet durable material, which cocooned my body. After all, our human bodies are made of the same biological building blocks as all the other life forms on our remarkable planet Earth. If any person so desired, he or she could train his or her body to do the same.

Inside my chrysalis all I could see was a furry, velvety wall of green-gray.

My higher functions ceased to operate at once.

Three months later on the dot, I stirred. I yawned and stretched and emerged from my chrysalis. I shook off the remnants, disabled the security device, and strode around the barn, feeling mighty fine.

My new body was covered in silvery sequins. They tinkled gaily as I strode, and made a merry music. For a second I thought I heard Alpine bells, and I thought of Glorious Jones.

Out the bright window of the hayloft, everything looked pretty in the world. I hugged myself. My sequins tinkled, gleaming in the gay sunlight.

I thought about how sad everyone would feel over not having sequins like mine. I considered the tragic, toxic incidents that would occur when teenagers decided to mimic my style, what terrible glues they would avail themselves of, what chemicals, how they might suffocate themselves with sequins or cause traffic accidents by reflecting their newfound glory into the eyes of oncoming drivers. So I squeezed my hindquarters into an industrial cheesemaking vat as if it were a washtub and began picking the sequins off myself one by one, hundreds of thousands of them, like brilliant little scabs, each scab an inestimable treasure.

In the midst of my project, I heard a rapping at the barn door, and the unmistakable voice of my cherubic landlady, Old

Mrs. Miggins.

I heard you stirring about, Mr. Awesome, she said through the closed door.

Yes ma'am, I called.

Mr. Awesome, everyone has gone and left me. Your fault, they say.

Why, Mrs. Miggins, whatever can you mean? I've been the most silent of tenants lo these many months.

Aye, that be true, said Old Mrs. Miggins, daughter of a famous whaler. But an unwholesome stench ye've made. Many's the boarder who has speculated as how ye might be a cannibal. It's none of my business, says I. I be from old New England stock. I don't like to be prying, don't ye know. He can cook up a whole crew of sailing men, aye, and tan their hides to boot, long as he keeps his quarters shipshape and pays me my little sum. Ah, but the smell, Mr. Awesome, the smell.

Old Mrs. Miggins, I have a wonderful idea. Why don't you brew me up a pot of your famous tea? I've been missing it all this time. We'll have some tea together and discuss all your worries in a civilized way. I'm quite sure amends can be made.

Tea. To be sure, ye've hit me weak spot, Mr. Awesome. Aye, ye be a large and cunning man.

As Mrs. Miggins tromped off to her kitchen, I continued to peel off my sequin skin. I admit to my disappointment in discovering that I had not grown a new wiener beneath the sequins. Still, the spot where my wiener had been was looking good, kind of like a slightly rounded piece of highly polished brass, like the blank crotch of a gloriously expensive doll.

When I had finished my task, the vat was filled to overflowing with sequins. I departed the barn for the cow pond, in the green surface of which I examined myself and saw that I looked none the worse for the wear. In fact, my cheeks were rosy and my hair was silky soft, and all in all I looked as if I had just completed a trip to a ritzy spa, where I had been immersed in the most enviable body lotions and hair-care products known to man.

It was time to expel some waste matter.

Here's what I do: I poop ambrosia.

It doesn't make a noise when it comes out, it doesn't have substance as such, its atomic weight is immeasurably small. I achieve it through a strict avoidance of beans, which are hard on the digestion. Immodest consumption of beans on one birthday in my youth resulted in a terrible explosion and a cloud of great toxicity that rendered a certain patch of farmland barren to this day. But I learned my lesson: no more beans. In consequence, if I poop on a city street, no one knows. All they notice is that things are better all of a sudden. There's a soft scent like cinnamon and autumn leaves and roasted peanuts and snow. A scent of childhood. Then generally everyone goes into a pleasant trance lasting up to twenty minutes.

So I went back to the barn, dispensing little intimations of soul along the way. I had a little left over when I got inside. I heard later that everyone said it was the best batch of cheese that the little dairy had ever produced.

The remnants of my chrysalis lay strewn about the floor like corn silk. I picked them up and wove them into a sheer and lovely bathrobe that barely covered my buttocks. I peeked out of the loft and saw Old Mrs. Miggins approaching, pushing our tea and all its trappings on a little cart before her.

I came out to greet her.

By the seven seas, Mr. Awesome, she exclaimed. I'll have to ask ye to cover yourself.

This is the most modest bathrobe I could produce. Besides, I thought you said that all the guests had departed.

Too true, too true. But Lord help us if someone should be ambling up the drive right now, looking for a respectable place to stay.

You cling to the old-fashioned values, Mrs. Miggins, and I can really get behind that, what with the craziness going on with the cable TV and miniskirts. You're a bulwark, Mrs. Miggins, that's what you are. In your own little corner of the globe, you're saving civilization, did you ever think of that?

I just try to keep a clean house, said Old Mrs. Miggins.

Precisely. And if we all did the same, it would be a giant step forward for humanity, ha ha, dear me, so to speak. As Candide concluded after his many trials and tribulations, We must tend our garden.

Old Mrs. Miggins spread a checkered blanket on the ground. Well, she said, ye've done right wonders getting rid of the stink, and I'm beholding to ye for that.

We're not as different as you think, Mrs. Miggins. Observe.

I raised my robe to let her see the smooth, shining space that my reproductive equipment had previously occupied.

The tea things went everywhere in a terrific smash.

Old Mrs. Miggins had become hypnotized by the glow of the perfectly bare and pristine metallic hillock of my crotch. I was afraid to drop my robe and cover it, due to the likely psychological effect, similar to that of awakening a sleepwalker.

What is it you're gaping at, Mrs. Miggins? I asked cautiously.

Her reply was somnambulistic: I see myself as a little girl, checking the lobster traps with Auntie Lucinda.

I concluded that Old Mrs. Miggins was suffering from a brain malfunction akin to epilepsy, brought on ocularly, no doubt, courtesy of the extreme shininess of the area upon which her gaze was affixed.

Now I see Grandfather playing his trombone in the attic.

Mrs. Miggins, I'm going to slowly lower my robe. Please remain calm.

I covered my mesmeric crotch. Old Mrs. Miggins emerged from her trance.

Glory be, what a terrible mess, she said of her scattered tea things.

Never you mind, Mrs. Miggins. Sit down and fan yourself and I'll take care of this.

You're always such a gentleman, Mr. Awesome, sir. Weren't we just discussing something?

Don't trouble your mind about it, dear, I said.

Yes, I suppose you're right. Does a body no good to fret. No good at all.

She lowered herself onto the checkered cloth and fanned herself as I had suggested.

I stooped to my task.

Mr. Awesome, a word to the wise, when ye bend yourself down like that I'm afraid you're in the way of showing your rear end to the whole of God's world.

I do beg your pardon, I said, rising.

Ah well, said Old Mrs. Miggins. Very odd, it's the kind of thing that would get me goat most days. Today I feel...

Relaxed? I said.

As though I'd just awakened from a green dream of the sea.

I cleaned up the remainder of the accident while Old Mrs. Miggins stared at my exposed bottom. It didn't seem to hypnotize her as the front view had, but neither did it agitate her. I suppose its effect was neutral.

Soon enough I had prepared a second afternoon tea for Old Mrs. Miggins and myself, and had brought it to table without incident. Old Mrs. Miggins, known all over New England for her exacting standards when it came to tea, declared it to be the most scrumptious and satisfying she had ever been served, as well as the most attractive in presentation.

Nothing could make me prouder, I said. The Japanese make a regular religion out of the tea service, you know. But I think they could learn something from you, Mrs. Miggins. If this tea passes muster at all, it is only because I myself have been the lucky recipient of such an education.

Oh, pshaw, said Mrs. Miggins.

Pshaw is my favorite word, I informed her.

Oh, pshaw, she said again.

We tittered discreetly.

Now, Mrs. Miggins, I don't suppose there were any calls for me these past few months?

Oh dearie me yes, a nice young man from the American Express. I hope you're in no financial trouble, Mr. Awesome…?

Not a bit, Mrs. Miggins. In fact, on that very subject, you mentioned earlier that the stench coming from my quarters had caused you to lose some business.

Think nothing of it, kind sir, after this dainty tea we've had and all these marvelous dainties.

I have a check here for you made out in the amount of a million dollars.

Saints preserve us, said Old Mrs. Miggins.

I trust that will cover your expenses.

I'm going to weep for a thousand years, said Old Mrs. Miggins, and indeed gave every appearance of fulfilling that surprising promise.

Also, I know how you like to sell spangly things to sewing aficionados via eBay, I said.

That I do, said Old Mrs. Miggins, a wreck of emotion.

You'll find a whole vat of such objects in your barn, wonderful little flakes made of a rare material, possibly platinum, or uranium.

You're too good to Old Mrs. Miggins, said Old Mrs. Miggins.

I took my leave of the remarkable old woman. Her wracking sobs of joy could be heard quite plainly at a distance of half a mile away. I stopped in at a fire station and alerted some kindly firemen to her condition.

44

I used the firehouse telephone to call American Express. I spoke with a polite young man named Ben, who confirmed that American Express had located the bones of Hernando de Soto, and wished to know where I wanted them delivered.

I'll just come by your corporate headquarters, Ben, and pick them up with my faithful red wagon, Ol' Tuffy.

Very good, sir. I feel compelled to mention that they are not bones, exactly. They are more like particles of muck and atoms of dust. Formerly bones.

I do appreciate your honesty and forthrightness, Ben. That's a rare trait in today's youth, and I commend you for it.

Well, sir, I was concerned for your happiness as a customer of American Express. After all, we are charging 140 million dollars to your account.

That's a large sum, Ben.

We had to use one of those special X-ray machines that looks underground, sir. Also, DNA technology. And in the end, sir, to tell you the truth, we couldn't find anything. So we hired a leading mathematician to determine what percentage of the air we breathe is actually composed of tiny specks of Hernando de Soto. Then, through a complicated series of formulae, we gathered the requisite amount of air and/or mud in several tanks to guarantee that at least one infinitesimal portion of

Hernando de Soto would be included. It was a very costly process, sir, and if I may be frank, perhaps not a successful or entirely honest one.

You're cute, Ben, the way you worry. You did the best you could, and that's all anyone can ask. May I inquire as to the health of your charming coworker Sally?

Sally left us, sir. She went into the pornography business, where she has made quite a splash as a successful actress. We were all surprised, because she had comported herself in a straitlaced manner up until that time.

It is not our place to judge her choices, I informed young Ben.

I would be the last to do so, sir. If I may speak freely, her work has had a profound influence on my life.

I secretly thought about all the good I had done.

Pulling Ol' Tuffy—laden with her haystack and numerous sparkling tanks containing some of the atoms of the legendary explorer—through the populous city streets of our nation, I was mistaken by many happy schoolchildren as a float in a marvelous parade.

Those innocent tykes could not have known the gloom that transpired behind my cheerful eyes. For I had opened the third envelope of Glorious Jones, and my next task was not such that a call to American Express could put it right.

THE MEANING OF LIFE

Who knows when life first acquired meaning? It would be presumptuous of us to think it was when the first caveman drew some kind of freaky buffalo on a wall with a stick, although that would be my guess.

But what about dinosaurs? Or amoebae? Who are we to dismiss their concerns?

I saw at once that my only choice was to travel back in time and witness the beginning of life itself. I would probably notice something that no one else had thought of before. And when I came back and told everybody, everybody would be like, Of course. Way to go. Here's a Nobel Prize.

I didn't need the money but medals are a fine honor, and fun to have around the house for conversation starters. Best of all, my acceptance speech might be posted on the internet, where Glorious Jones was bound to see. It couldn't hurt to remind her I was out there in the world, giving it my best shot.

But how might time travel be accomplished? I considered the literature. A potable drug in Daphne du Maurier, a truck fueled by psychedelic mushrooms in Charles McNair, a machine in H. G. Wells, an oxygen-annihilating chemical in Flann O'Brien, a bump on the head in Mark Twain, a time tunnel in the TV series *The Time Tunnel*, and a quantum leap in the TV series *Quantum Leap*.

I was, by trade and inclination, a robot maker extraordinaire, and many laymen believe that if one can build a robot, one can build anything. But a time machine required a certain specialization that I did not possess. That didn't make me feel worse about myself as a human being, or any less proud of my numerous and incredible accomplishments, or any less handsome and awesomely put together. If anything, my willingness to admit I was not perfect made me even more perfect than I had previously expected.

Given my limitations, I determined to focus upon the least technologically challenging of time-travel methods. I had discovered during my adventure with Scrawny and his friends that psychedelic mushrooms did nothing for me, but even I was not immune to the old-fashioned bump on the head. I recalled that Twain's Hank Morgan had made it back to Arthurian times via a crowbar to the skull.

But I was bigger and tougher and going farther back.

I needed to be shot in the head with a cannonball.

Needless to say, such an operation would require a marksman of considerable skill.

I am such a marksman, but the sad fact remains that one cannot properly shoot oneself in the head with a cannon.

So there I stood, having rushed with the heedlessness that often accompanies brilliance, on the exact geographical point where Arizona, New Mexico, Colorado, and Utah meet, where dinosaurs had roamed in abundance in times of yore, when I realized that I had dismantled the only being who could help me achieve my aim, and left him stuffed in a New England butter churn.

I walked back to Vermont. I was in such a hurry that it took me only a day and a half.

The Miggins place appeared to have suffered hard times. The doors were wide open and the furniture scattered on the lawn, as if in preparation for an estate sale. I feared the worst. I got down on all fours, the better to call to anyone within.

Hello? I said. Hello?

A chilly, beautiful woman with a mannish haircut emerged from the dark mouth of the house, mannish clothing tight against her slim body.

May I help you? she said.

I'm looking for Old Mrs. Miggins, I said.

I'm her niece. Dottie Flambeau.

I pondered the icy eyes of Dottie Flambeau.

And where is the dear old girl? I said.

Someone gave her a million dollars, said Dottie Flambeau.

That would be me.

Your gift rendered her catatonic. As a psychologist, I concluded that she was quite literally paralyzed by happiness. It's unlikely that she will ever recover from your so-called generosity. We are selling off all her belongings so that she can get the care she needs.

Why not just cash the check? I asked.

In her catatonia, she was not able to endorse it.

So you're into psychology, I said.

Yes, I'm a trained psychologist.

Isn't that something. You look just like the famous movie actress Lindsay Crouse, who played a psychologist in the film *House of Games*, written and directed by her then-husband, David Mamet. You also share her mannered, flat inflection, so effective when delivering clipped, stylized dialogue of a Mametesque variety.

So I've been told, said Dottie Flambeau. I don't care for the cinema.

One night at the movies with me and you'd change your tune, sweet cheeks, I said.

Dottie Flambeau started at my flirtatiousness.

Don't worry, it was an icebreaker, I said. I know you're married, and I so respect the sanctity of that and stuff. Your last name, Flambeau, is not characteristic of this region. I would say you probably married a gentleman from Louisiana.

Astounding, said Dottie Flambeau. It's like you can see right inside of me. You understand me better than my husband does. Listen, would you mind spending an hour or so with me, talking about my sexual dysfunction? I can take this sheet off the couch here in the yard and lie down while you plumb my psyche.

I'm not a doctor, I said.

What's that, doctor? You'd like me to undress? Very well. I want you to examine the shapely runnel of my back.

With that she whipped off her top, revealing her loveliness.

Please, Dottie, think of your family, I said.

Touch my runnel, she said.

I declined. But I did snort a small, hot breath in the direction of her runnel. I had hoped merely to humor her, but the instant that my breath made contact with her skin she convulsed again and again with an orgasm of devastating magnitude.

As a few residual spasms left her quivering on the porch, I dashed to the barn to retrieve the butter churn containing the pieces of Jimmy.

When I stopped by to check on her, Dottie Flambeau was fully dressed and smoking a cigarette of tobacco. She looked quite cool and composed given her recent exertions.

That butter churn belongs to my poor aunt, she said.

It contains some personal property belonging to me, I said.

Dump it out, she said.

I did as she required. Jimmy lay in a pile at my feet.

What's that? she said. A broken-down old washing machine?

Jimmy, my robot ward, I said.

Allow me, she said.

To my astonishment, Dottie Flambeau reassembled Jimmy in a matter of minutes.

You didn't tell me you were an expert in robotics, I said.

A few minutes ago I wasn't, said Dottie Flambeau. It was that orgasm you gave me. As best as I can theorize without further tests, it opened up an unused portion of my pineal gland, unleashing my hidden talents.

Well, I'm glad it worked out, I said. And thanks for fixing Jimmy, my robot ward.

Mother, said Jimmy.

Dottie and I shared a chuckle at that.

Listen, she said, you'd be doing me a big favor if you could assist me with some more tests. I could write up the results in a scientific journal and buy my husband a bass boat with all the money I make.

And treat yourself to something nice, I said.

I saw a look in her eyes that I had never earned from Glorious Jones.

Jimmy flew back to Louisiana with Dottie Flambeau. I ran along under the plane, waving.

In a few months, Dottie had set up a kind of clinic where I breathed on people's backs and gave them orgasms. Each person was observed to exhibit some kind of material improvement.

Gertrude sang in a lovely contralto.

Annabel became an expert in medieval Russian iconography.

Haley displayed a knack for ventriloquism bordering on the uncanny.

Rex's cholesterol was lowered by thirty-two points.

Betty spoke perfect Portuguese.

Jon produced a series of scathing political cartoons.

Kim excelled in ballroom dancing.

Angel Sue took up the timbales.

Michelle could tell what animals were thinking.

Philip made a jukebox play by striking it with the palm of his hand.

Dottie took copious notes on my technique, although she refused to undergo a second orgasm, which she felt might subvert her scientific objectivity. She wrote up her findings in a well-received article entitled "Harnessing the Psychic Power of the Orgasm through Non-Tactile Pineal Massage," published in the winter issue of *Labia: The Johns Hopkins Journal of Sexiness.*

In the evening, after a day of hard work at the clinic, Dottie Flambeau and I would return to her comfortable home and have dinner with her husband, Charlie, who was very dull in a nice way. Often I would remark to him, You know, Charlie, it's a real blessing to be like you.

Charlie, at great expense to himself, and as a birthday gift to his wife, had had the roof of their home removed by a construction crew so that Dottie and I could feel closer to one another and share our secrets and build our relationship through long conversations, and so I could watch her as she slept or took a bath.

I sat in their backyard, on the crushed remains of Charlie's toolshed, where he had formerly liked to go tinker with lawn mowers. When it stormed I hunkered over the little family and kept them dry. In fact, I tended to loom at all times and it made Charlie adorably self-conscious. Many a time as he sat on the toilet I would explain to him how to lighten up and enjoy what life offered.

Charlie worked on an oilrig and was gone a lot. Even when at home he retired early, leaving Dottie and myself to cozy up on the couch. Extending my index and middle fingers as if they were legs, I would cause my right hand to "sit" on the couch in the posture of a person. Sometimes I would "cross" my "legs" in a cute manner, which was always a big hit. Then there was the time Dottie tried to manicure my nails with a power sander and Charlie came in and took over because it was "man's work." Oh, Charlie. How simpleminded you were, and I mean that in an awesome way. Dottie had quite a time pretending my hand was a lover against whom she could rub her socked feet as we watched hour after hour of *Project Runway* on the extremely highbrow Bravo channel. Sometimes I stuck out my thumb and she nestled in the whorl of my fingerprint.

I recall one night in particular. We were sated, full of biscuits, high-end boutique-style root beer, and organic pea soup, and Charlie was snoring quite loudly in the other room (I could look down and see him there all in a tangle of sheets) and I was smoking an antique pipe with a very long stem and wearing a monocle for laughs and Dottie was drinking rosehip tea of exquisite quality and her feet were rubbing a mile a minute and a fire snapped its bright fingers at us from the fireplace and the fish were doing their thing in the fish tank, which put the most quizzical expression on the new puppy's face.

Maybe this is what it's all about, I said. Not just running around finding stuff and piling it in my wagon.

I must admit that I sank into a kind of routine with Dottie Flambeau and good old Charlie, the salt of the earth. I felt bad about sitting on his toolshed, so I showed him how to pursue a new hobby by setting up an apiary in the capacious bed of Ol' Tuffy. He was allergic to bees and spent a year hovering near death but everything turned out all right and later I ribbed him about it.

Charlie, why didn't you mention you were allergic to bees?

I thought an apiary is where you kept apes, he said.

Oh, Charlie, you wonderful hick.

Our agreeable laughter rang through the night.

I walked around some whole days like I was nothing but an ordinary dude. And I guess I was hypnotized or acclimated or something, because I liked it a lot.

47

The time came for another round of tests on Dottie's subjects, and another set of orgasms. The results were not encouraging.

Haley had double vision.

Annabel developed Tourette's syndrome.

Gertrude hallucinated all the time.

Philip experienced bedwetting and significant memory loss.

Michelle complained of feminine itching.

Angel Sue sat in the empty bathtub and nicked herself repeatedly with a box cutter.

Kim displayed signs of pyromania.

Jon suffered from night terrors.

Betty became cynical.

Rex wept blood and later died.

This called into question some of the findings in Dottie's original article, which put her in academic disrepute.

And yet our subjects craved more. They were having trouble with their marriages and serious relationships. Normal human orgasms weren't good enough for them anymore.

Can't you see where this is heading? I asked. See, you got greedy. You lost sight of what was really important, like your loved ones, for example, not some magic orgasm that made you feel better than you ever felt in your life. The magic orgasm is inside your hearts, it's whatever makes you special, it's whatever you want it to be.

That blew their freaking minds. They were like, Thanks, you're the best psychiatrist in the world.

Everybody went home to give it one last shot with their significant others. I watched them go with a certain expression on my face.

48

That night was a somber one in the Flambeau household. I barely picked at my crawfish étouffée. Charlie had made dinner, and he was ever so proud. He had even hired one of his construction worker friends to deliver it to my mouth in the scoop of a bulldozer. But I demurred.

What's the matter, don't you like it?

It's fine, Charlie. I guess I just don't have much of an appetite.

But it's Christmas Eve, it is, guv'nuh. (Charlie always tried to lighten tough moments by pretending to be a cockney foundling.)

I've been here almost six years, Charlie. I never said I could stay forever. What I said about orgasms today has really got me reevaluating my situation.

Charlie's lip began to tremble. He was a weak man, and there's nothing wrong with that. Charlie was the kind of guy who practically begged somebody to come along and make free and easy with his wife. It was his slouched demeanor, and the way his gut poked out in mournful resignation. And the pockmarks.

Meanwhile, Dottie affected a crisp stoicism. Even the puppy, which by now had grown into a dog, displayed anthropomorphic sadness, tilting his head this way and that. I knew we were just ascribing human emotions to him, what the literary crowd calls *the pathetic fallacy*, but gosh it was a solemn night, with the blue lights twinkling on the tree.

I'll have a blue Christmas without you, guv'nuh, said Charlie, and we all burst into tears, including the dog, the bulldozer operator, and, it seemed, the fish in the aquarium. In the garbage pail, the black eyes of the crawfish heads appeared to glisten with emotion. Only Dottie remained unaffected. I commented on the fact.

This is the way I express despair, she said, expressing nothing.

It occurred to me that we're all different in this crazy world. I had learned a lot in Louisiana. Especially a little something about the importance of being yourself. But now it was time to move on. I had become too comfortable. Maybe I had been looking for the meaning of life all along without knowing it. But it wasn't here, not for me.

Come on, Jimmy, I said. I dislodged him from his place under the sink, where we had been using him as a garbage disposal unit since my arrival.

He couldn't answer, because his vocalization center had naturally been unplugged for the sake of convenience.

49

I crossed some famous bridge in Louisiana while the sun went down in the water, throwing off color. What a sight I must have made from afar, a majestic silhouette pulling my wagon behind me, hunched over with determination and perhaps a twinge of regret, Jimmy, my robot ward, riding along with a loaded cannon ready to pop.

To be technical it was carronade, creaky, rotten Revolutionary War cannonry named for its manufacture in Carron, Scotland, infamously difficult to aim, but it was all we had been able to find in the antique shops of New Orleans. I convinced myself that its slightly lower velocity might even be preferable for safety purposes. Accuracy was an unfortunate sacrifice.

I strode past truck stops, water towers, strip malls, nice yards, and things that looked broken, pausing only to drink from an oversize promotional novelty thermos filled with Pimm's Cups. At last we reached Chaco Canyon National Historical Park.

I lifted Jimmy out of the wagon, set him up behind the cannon, and reactivated his audio capabilities.

Now, Jimmy, I said, I want you to be particularly careful. Make sure you get me square in the head, because as you know, my one vulnerability is being shot in the navel with a cannon. Don't tell anybody.

Oh, I'm very aware of that, said Jimmy, my robot ward.

That's weird, Jimmy. I didn't program you with vocal inflections, yet I could swear that you just spoke with a menacing edge.

That does not compute, said Jimmy.

Exactly, Jimmy. Personality would be a prerequisite. Ol' Tuffy here [I patted the side of my famous red wagon] has more of a personality than you do. I recognize the irrationality of my feeling yet I cannot deny its significance. Sometimes as I make my way across this broad nation, towing her behind, I tell her the innermost secrets of my breaking heart, isn't that right, Ol' Tuffy, isn't that right, old girl [more patting here]? I appreciate the foolishness of the sentiment, yet I cannot help feeling that Ol' Tuffy is the best and most loyal friend I have ever had.

I made ready, hands on hips, legs apart, sporting a look of proud defiance for some reason. I guess it just felt right.

Jimmy shot me in the navel.

I went down.

When I woke up I had developed amnesia. I recognized the symptoms of this, the most common disease in the United States of America, from a number of bestselling experimental literary novels concerned with the human condition and the limitations of language itself. Strangely, though I remembered those novels word for word I could not remember anything about myself, aside from the vague notion that I needed to find something.

I appeared to have been deposited in the Florida Everglades. Someone had gone to the trouble of dressing me in a natty pinstriped suit and placing a fresh peppermint-striped camellia bush in my lapel.

When I sat up I felt an abrasiveness through my silk shirt. I reached into the inner pocket of my jacket and pulled out a sheet of notebook paper—not from a giant notebook, either, but from a very tiny notebook, even by regular notebook standards. Yet the great sensitivity of my nipples—a million times more sensitive than ordinary human nipples, according to a study undertaken by the Mayo Clinic at my request—was such that I had felt it rubbing against me. Yes, my nipples were a curse as much as a blessing but I could not imagine life without them.

I read at the top of the page:

Things to Find

Just as I thought, I thought.

The list seemed to consist of five items, the first four of which had been crossed off with a magic marker of such efficacy that I could not make out a single word.

Doesn't matter, I told myself. Obviously I am good at finding things. And when I find this final thing perhaps everything will click into place and my memory will be restored. I believe that's the way it usually works. But I don't remember.

I could not have realized at the time that the list was a forgery and I was playing into the hands of a brilliant rival. Had I only known to check, I would have found that my actual list, sweetly sealed in its various epistolary caskets, was gone.

Under the circumstances, however, the only course of action was to complete the mission with which I had been charged.

A MARACA

That sounds like an easy one, I said to a flock of strange albino birds, which rose into the swampy air as one.

And so I walked around the United States of America until I came to a Mexican restaurant.

No maraca here, sir.

Such was the answer I received at the first establishment I visited, and the tenth, and the fiftieth, and all the ones in between.

Odd, I thought. Almost as if someone had divested the United States of America of its maracas. But why?

Well, I said to myself, I'll just try about fifty or a hundred more and then I'll head over the border to Mexico.

In St. Paul, Minnesota, one of America's famed Twin Cities, I got on my hands and knees and visited the drive-thru of a yellow stucco place called, with hints of promise, Maraca Joe's.

Pardon me, I said, bending my head to the speaker implanted in the drive-up menu. I'm required to locate and obtain a maraca. I don't suppose you'd have one, for decoration, with which you would be willing to part?

I just started here, said the voice of a hapless trainee.

I tell you what. Why don't I just come around to the window so we can discuss it in person? I like to see the man I'm talking to. What's your name, son?

You need to order something, sir. The drive-thru is not made for chitchat. We can get in trouble for that, and I'm still like on probation and stuff.

Point well taken. It sounds as if you've memorized your training manual from top to bottom, and I commend you. One thousand Cokes, please. Light ice.

It seems like you're trying to fool me.

Not at all. I assure you I would like one thousand Cokes and I am quite willing to pay.

What size would you like those Cokes?

Medium. And don't forget, I want light ice.

Okay. Please drive around.

About that maraca, I said, when I reached the window.

I'm new here, the boy said to my one eye peeping in.

And you don't wish to muddle things up by giving away the store, am I right, Jeremy? [I had read his nametag.]

Jeremy laughed, taken with my easygoing manner, which put him at ease.

I guess that's right, he said. You seem nice and all, but…

Say no more, Jeremy. Say no more. You're doing a bang-up job, and I wouldn't doubt that you'll soon be up for a big promotion. I'd like to speak to your manager, Jeremy.

She's not here today. Do you want to talk to Doug?

I have no earthly idea who this Doug person is, Jeremy, but no, I feel no need to speak to him.

He's like the manager when Sherry's not here.

But he's not really the manager, is he, Jeremy?

No. Sherry is.

The man named Doug appeared, a redfaced fellow with coppery hair and glasses, I would say twenty-six years of age and bound to have a stroke by forty. Not that he was portly, indeed he was slender, but the signs of apoplexy were all about him.

What's the holdup here? said Doug. What's all this crud about one thousand medium Cokes?

He wants to like borrow a maraca, said Jeremy. Do we have any? I don't even know if we have any.

Are you going to make a serious order, sir? said Doug. There are other people who would like to pick up their food.

You make a good point, Doug. We need to consider their feelings, the feelings of others.

You're not some inspector from corporate, are you? said Doug.

Well, I wouldn't be likely to admit it if I were, would I,

Doug? That's a good thought you had, though. That's an interesting thing for you to ponder. Ordering a thousand Cokes to see if you're on your toes. I'm going to go out back by the trash, okay, Doug? And I'm going to wait there for ten minutes. If you don't join me within that time, Doug, I'm going to assume that you don't care to speak with me, or to find out what kind of fascinating things I might have to say.

I sat with my knees hugged to my chest and waited. I knew he would come. In addition to his understandable need to control his tiny kingdom, I had sensed that Doug was at heart a businessman, someone who could not resist hearing an intriguing proposition.

What's your game? he said. You must want me to pay you to stand out front and attract customers. Well, let's hear it. It stinks back here and I got things to do.

Do you think I'm a sharpie, young Doug? Some kind of scammer? A lurker among the trash bins, on the prowl? I want you to dig this awesome pinstriped suit, Doug. You have to ask yourself, what kind of dude is together enough to slide into a bitching set of togs like these? A human peacock, Doug. A man of confidence, and a man who inspires confidence, but not a confidence man. I'm going to lay it on the line for you, Doug. I'm going to be vulnerable and admit something. I don't even know where this get-up came from. Somebody dressed me in it while I was asleep. Somebody saw me asleep, Doug, and thought, This dude deserves to look like a million bucks, and dressed me accordingly, at no cost to me. That's the kind of loyalty I inspire, Doug. [By subtly repeating his name, I was winning him over through psychology and rhetoric.] Now don't you want to do business with a serious player like me? A man of flash and pizzazz? [Here I opened the jacket to reveal the pink satin lining.] Well? You like what you see, Doug? Is it speaking to you?

It sucks without a hat, said Doug.

The word HAT struck me in the pit of my biology.

Why did you say that, Doug? Some part of my damaged memory is troubled. [Here I felt my head for a hat that wasn't there. My derby shone before me in the ether, yes, I remembered it, but could not grasp its significance.] Let me see if I can explain it for you, this feeling I just got. Did you go to college, Doug?

Though he was silent, I could tell from his expression that he had not enjoyed the benefits of a higher education.

That's perfectly okay, Doug. I want you to respect yourself anyway. There is a lot to be said for the school of hard knocks. And the references I'm going to make are likely embedded in our popular culture, so you will understand them instinctually, like an iguana. When you mentioned my absent hat, Doug, something flashed for me, like when that dude was all, Is this a dagger I see before me? or when that other dude saw the Holy Grail and he was like, Can I touch it? but it disappeared, and I think he heard the Voice of God saying, No way, dude, no way. Are you with me so far?

Yes, Doug lied.

What I'm getting at, Doug, is that you seem to know something I don't know. Why else would you mention a hat? There is no insult intended, Doug, when I observe your manager's uniform of ecru Dacron, with its soiled epaulets, and speculate that you are not a fashion expert. Some shadowy figure has prepared you for our meeting. Somehow, you knew I was coming. I'll be one hundred percent frank right now, Doug, I have amnesia and there's a lot of stuff I'm fuzzy on. So you might think you have some kind of advantage, like you're putting one over on me, teasing me or baiting me, making hints about my special derby that you think I can't remember. It probably makes you feel big and important, and those are compelling emotions, Doug, no one will deny it. It feels good to be special. But I'm going to tell you something that maybe you don't know, Doug. Amnesia can be frustrating. It can make a person vulnerable and confused. I'm sure you've felt that way before, Doug, we all have. It's a natural part of growing up. But right now, Doug [here I rose], I'm having a childish reaction, and you know, I just want to break something.

I kicked four trash bins out of the way and they went sailing into the clouds one by one. I then stepped over to Maraca Joe's and punched through the roof. I happened to reach into the men's room, where I tore holes in the foam-colored tile, yanked out great fistfuls of pipe. Water and sewage sprayed everywhere. Big, apocalyptic swarms of zinc dust exploded in the air. I bellowed like a wounded bull.

My time has come to die, said Doug. He was upset.

What do you know, Doug? What is it that you know?

He trembled on his knees before me.

Are you from corporate? he said.

No, Doug. I'm a friend. A friend who's interested in acquiring a maraca.

We only had one, said Doug.

Where is it?

Gone, said Doug.

Gone where?

I'm not supposed to say. I swore not to tell. If Sherry knew…

Who was it, Doug? Who wanted the maraca?

I can't. I can't reveal anything about their identity. He said…

He or she, if you intend to be secretive, I reminded Doug.

He or she said that he'd kill me if I told anybody. If Sherry finds out she'll fire my ass. But I don't want to die. I have dreams of being a scuba diver.

Oh, Doug. It's okay to be scared. It's okay to have dreams.

Wait, there's something else. He—he or she—told me that a giant would come looking for a maraca. A giant without a hat. And that I should give them this.

With that Doug produced in his shaky hands, from the folds of his Dacron apron, my packet of instructional letters, the riband bedraggled, each envelope ravished, roughly opened and smudged.

I imbibed the faded perfume of Glorious Jones.

My memory was restored.

Did I have an enemy? Someone who had dressed me in pin-stripes, yet derbyless, to make me feel ridiculous and alone?

Someone broken by the same spiritual crisis as mine, at the exact same time, coincidentally (in every sense of that adverb) in need of the same remedy? Someone who would do anything to know the contents of my precious list? It seemed to be the only logical answer. A lumbering hobo ogre, driven by nothing but the need in his red pig eyes, the hole in his core, a poxy man enrobed with the stink of the grave.

Who else but a being with concomitant power would be able to manipulate my actions in such a fashion? Perhaps he had programmed me to forget the true nature of my quest by means of a phonographic record played over and over as I slumbered in unconsciousness. Yes, I reached inside my right ear and pulled out a top-of-the-line boom box with a fifty-CD changer. I had been brainwashed. But now I was free.

We thought alike, he and I. The grudging admiration I had seen displayed by police detectives for their serial killer adversaries in so many wonderful Hollywood melodramas—now I felt it for the first time, pulsing in my throat.

What of the scientists who had spirited away my wiener? Might they have cloned me from the wiener up? Might my adversary be myself? Certainly we have all enjoyed trick endings, such as when Brad Pitt and Edward Norton turn out to be the same person, or Mickey Rourke is hot on the trail of himself, or John Cusack only exists in somebody's head.

My enemy, whoever he was, had a head start, of this much I was convinced. It would have taken him some time to confiscate the maracas of our land but no doubt he had calculated the consequences and found them to be worth the trouble. This type of entity would probably not mind at all the idea of stealing my red wagon full of hard-won treats. Or, if he thought he *was* me, mightn't he claim Ol' Tuffy with a degree of reasonableness that even I would be hard pressed to counter? After all, who is to say who is who these days? Identity has been in flux since about 1946, as nearly everyone who has published a book with a university press agrees.

I hurried back to Chaco Canyon, where I found Ol' Tuffy

and her contents undisturbed. Good news—but my next move had me stymied. I had not yet found the meaning of life. I decided to seek insight where Old Mrs. Miggins had found it in abundance. This, I felt sure, was a resource that my rival did not, could not, possess.

There were difficulties, to be sure. How might one stare, head-on and right side up, at one's own crotch? Certainly mirrors would be employed, most likely a complex system of them, but would the mirror image achieve the same effect as the actual, physical presence of that shiny spot? Or would the light from the mirrors adversely affect the firing of whatever neurons were responsible for the power of my special place?

Second, I could understand how other people could get gaga over an unexpected glimpse of my anatomy, and how that might trigger certain physiological reactions bordering on the preternatural. But I was quite familiar—spiritually and physically, through many hours of healthful and innocent self-play— with my killer bod in all its many manifestations, and doubted, therefore, that anything it did could surprise me.

One thing is certain. All the philosophizing about principles and footling around in the world won't find you the meaning of life. I made the necessary preparations to take a good, hard, long, tender, contemplative gander at my own astonishing crotch.

✌

I traveled to an island off the coast of South Carolina, where I
rented a decrepit amusement park for my own personal use.

Sic transit gloria mundi. Such was the nature of my thoughts
in the dead tongue of Latin as I traversed the wrecked bounty of
the forgotten playground.

Methinks I detect the cries of ghostly children, I said with
a touch of ironical pretense.

Had there been a companion with me, however, I knew
that said companion would have soon begun to quake in fear,
beset by auditory hallucinations of creepy children singing a
wordless, out-of-tune jump rope rhyme, for such is the bedev-
ilment of suggestibility in the human brain.

Then I would have calmed my friend, saying, No, see, that
is just the wind wheezing through the bent calliope, or That is
just the natural settling of the carousel upon its poor founda-
tions, or That is just the hooting of the baby owls nesting in the
broken eye sockets of the giant clown.

It was the darkest and spookiest hour of the night, yet I had
no need of a flashlight. In the first place, very little on this earth
gives me concern of bodily injury. Secondly, my catlike senses.
It might be said as truly of me as of the eighteenth-century poet
and bedlamite Christopher Smart's cat Jeoffry that "he counteracts the powers of darkness by his electrical skin and glaring

eyes, / For he counteracts the Devil, who is death, by brisking about the life."

I negotiated the collapsed labyrinth of the hall of mirrors, looking for the sweet spot. My algebraic equations had informed me that if I could just find a place with enough mirrors, and shards of mirrors, it would be quite possible to find that nexus where I would be surrounded by myriad images of my own crotch, where I could look around and see nothing but my own shining bump of purest emptiness.

Ah, here. The meeting place. The long-anticipated encounter, perhaps set in motion by the action of a couple of particles of carbon at the beginning of time itself. I pulled down my pants. All around me, glinting, gathering every hint of light and casting it back at my face in glory, everywhere I looked, shone a thousand reflected crotches, my crotches, my crotch, gazing back at me, like a diamond mine, like a holy creature with a thousand eyes, guarding the throne of God.

And then it happened. Everything was concentrated in a pinpoint of light, and suddenly I could see into it. It was not that the pinpoint became larger, or that I drew closer to it, either spiritually or physically; it was simply that I could *see*. I saw the marriage of Glorious Jones to another man. I saw her swell with child. I saw the earth melting like a ball of wax.

$\mathcal{JJ}$

There followed a period of what alien abductees call lost time.

I awoke, flat on my back, at the fairgrounds, in the carnival dirt, near the cockeyed Ferris wheel, the sun peeking over its summit. My pants were missing. A group of curious demolition workers were taking turns staring at my spot of mystery.

One of them said something I could not understand. In any case, his assertion—apparently rendered in the language of Spanish, the one language in the world with which I am unacquainted—earned him a lighthearted mocking from his compatriots, one of whom shoved him aside with surprising roughness to get his own look.

This second fellow immediately entered a state of near catatonia.

Excuse me, gentlemen, I said, covering my crotch with my hands. Have you seen my pants?

The gazer fell upon his rump, raising a great cloud of dust. His buddies seemed to get a big kick out of his antics.

They babbled at me in their strange language, which was impossible to understand.

These were hardworking men of good cheer, and now that I had awakened, they could not have been more solicitous as to my comfort. First, they fitted me with a makeshift pair of pants, fashioned pell-mell from a couple of circus tents—gaudy, but practicable, and tenderly proffered. Next, I was guided to the lunchwagon, where the quantities of coffee and doughnuts that I was able to consume roused awe and admiration.

Then I felt the need to be alone, such are my many moods.

I thanked my new friends for their hospitality and excused myself.

I wandered to the far side of the park, where I leaned against the great central stalk of the ruined Tilt-A-Whirl.

In despair I fingered my ravaged envelope. The meaning of life? Ha. All my crotch had revealed to me was a null. How could I hope to find something that had never existed?

I could see, across a distance of several furlongs, the workmen gathering to demolish a large sepulchral box of ragged green wood, painted on each side with a red question mark.

As I observed them I felt like Walt Whitman or Carl Sandburg or Thomas Hart Benton or some other salt-of-the-earth type dude who could really get into the idea of other dudes swinging a hammer, especially some brown dudes acquainted with that golden orb the sun.

They went after the box with sledges and crowbars and hatchets and chisels, and, when all that failed, plastic explosives. The box looked battered—had looked that way when they started—but it was a good box and nothing they could do to it made the least dent or impression. It just stood there in its boxiness.

Though I valued the stoic human enterprise of the little workingmen scurrying about like so many insects, I felt a more visceral connection to the sullen stance of the silent and impenetrable box.

Wow, I said to myself. That box seems as impenetrable as the meaning of life itself.

Of course.

Fellas, I shouted. Dudes. Hold up.

But the workingmen did not hear me, having crammed cotton into their sensitive ears prior to setting off what they intended as their most devastating explosion yet. They cowered behind a fallen cast-iron figure of a bull elephant, their goggles and other safety equipment securely in place.

I arrived just as the bomb detonated. The workers were aghast and filled with wonderment to see me stride through the smoke of their explosion, shrugging off the shower of shrapnel like a Saint Bernard shaking himself dry after the lightest of summer drizzles.

I was delighted to see, as the smoke cleared, that the box remained intact.

What's up with this box? I asked.

They seemed to answer me, though I could not understand them.

I'm going to expostulate that in happier times some dude in a straw hat and striped jacket would stand up here waving a cane at it, am I right? Offering ten thousand crisp American dollars for the man, woman, or child who can penetrate the Box of Mystery. Something like that? A rigged carny game. Ingenious. What does it hold? No one knows. And yet for that very reason it just might hold the answer to all my troubles. Right, boys?

Once more their grunts and barks were beneath my comprehension, but I was proud of them for being able to tell where to jump in—namely, at my dramatic pauses.

I'm going to take that box and put it in my little red wagon, I said.

The men were amazed by the musical sound of my words, which they could never fathom, but more so by my manliness, which was universal. They had a good laugh from the sunshine and enjoyment I had brought into their spirit-crushing lives as usual. But when I made a move toward the box, they formed a line before me.

Ah, but it serves a need and I must have it. I don't expect you boys to understand this, but consider what the philosopher W. V. Quine said about Borges's impossibly vast universal library: that it could be reduced to two slips of paper, one containing a dot and the other a dash. Morse code, get it, boys? Who's with me? Perhaps you'd prefer to think of it in the binary terms of our computer age.

Most of my sad new chums traced circles in the dirt with the steel-reinforced toes of their practical boots, embarrassed by their inability to get the heavy stuff I was laying on them.

That's precisely the reaction I was looking for, I said. You boys have made me the happiest man on earth. Now, I don't know about you, but I used to have a major problem with Wittgenstein. Like, remember when he was all, There's no guarantee that the sun will come up tomorrow, so we cannot state that the sun will come up tomorrow? And I was like, Come on, Witty. If the sun doesn't come up tomorrow we'll all be in a crazy fix anyway. So who's going to care what you said yesterday? For all practical purposes, if there's anyone around to confirm that the sun came up, it will be true. And if the sun doesn't come up, true or false won't matter, because either instantly or shortly thereafter, no one will be around to correct you. So when people ask me if I've found the meaning of life I'm going to say, It's in this impenetrable box. And whatever they say next, I'll say, Exactly. And that will blow their minds. Like, what if they say, Prove it. I'll say, Exactly. Or what if they say, No it isn't. I'll say, Exactly. Consider the question mark painted on this box, representing what Charles Ives called "The Unanswered Question." The flutes were all atwitter while the strings embodied the silent, spinning stars. Who said that architecture was like frozen music? Anybody? Anybody? Okay, I see some confused faces. Is everybody still with me?

One cocky lad piped up: Sure I get it.

Really? I said.

Yeah, sure, yeah, I speak a little English. It's like this. So…oh, hell no, mister, I don't get it.

I understood this young man's attitude. He wanted to be in on the big questions of life, but nobody had invited him to the party. It was the inequitable system I had read so much about. I would have liked to explain the whole thing to him right then and there, but I was in a race, most likely with an evil doppel-ganger, and the clock was ticking.

I'll just take this and be going, then, I said. Thank you for your time, and the delicious snacks. Also, this enormous canvas diaper which you whipped together in a real jiffy. I doubt there are very many tenured professors at leading universities who could have done a comparable job, so you certainly have that going for you if nothing else, and I mean that from the heart.

I pointed at my heart. Everyone was excited to recognize the universal symbol.

They seemed inclined to let me have the box, with the exception of the cocky young man, who had the name Joaquin sewn neatly into an oval on the left pap of his uniform.

I can see your anger at the bosses and big men of this world, Joaquin, I said. And I support you one hundred percent. Although I am a big man, I am not a bossman. But has it occurred to you that you are conforming to the unseen bossman's expectations—the bossman reclining, no doubt, upon a divan at this very moment, in his sun-dappled study, drinking China tea?

He will never miss this box.

Some of the men jabbered at Joaquin, appearing to take my side. He jabbered back at them in their unfamiliar tongue.

I hated to see persons of the same meager wage-earning potential going at one another uncharitably, so I decided to play peacemaker.

Now, boys, I said. You must admit that Joaquin has a fair point. This box is not mine to take. Often we see that those most hurt by the power structure of a given society are its staunchest defenders, and Joaquin is no exception. If I am understanding your exotic traditions correctly, gentlemanly combat is indicated. I intend to beat you up according to the rules of sportsmanship. Afterward, if any one of you is left standing, you may keep your silly box.

Joaquin translated my words to them, which had the desired effect. By insulting the box, in which they seemed to take some proprietary pride as its potential destroyers (and therefore protectors), and by furthermore impugning their masculinity, I had found the exceedingly cute underbelly of their particular foreign brand of toughness.

One by one, they marched up to fight me as their fellows stood around us in a big circle, cheering along their representative of the moment.

My first little challenger approached marionette-like in a classic nineteenth-century boxing stance. I bent low and flicked him away through an action of my middle finger and thumb. We all watched as he rocketed over the horizon, his boots bursting into flames. I was as surprised as anyone.

I made a mental note to calibrate my future efforts with more care.

I must say that I was pleased to see the next fellow come at me with no less enthusiasm than his recently launched brother. I had to admit a certain grudging admiration for this mysterious and savage people with their many colorful traditions of honor. There it was again, grudging admiration, quite the nicest sensation that I had ever felt, aside from the warmth of Glorious Jones. I lifted the fellow by the scruff of the neck and deposited him on a jagged iron beam at the pinnacle of a mangled rollercoaster.

I reached down and picked up three or four more in my fist, their little heads poking out from between my knuckles. As I was considering what to do with them, they cleverly wriggled out of their shirts, falling from what was, for them, a great height, smashing their bones and bruising themselves both internally and externally. This rugged band dragged themselves to the sidelines and nursed one another's contusions. All the while I was holding off another one with a finger to the top of his head. His arms and legs flailed as he tried to move forward.

It occurred to me how sad he must feel. Plus, I was getting a backache from all the bending over. I rose and let him come at me, raising my foot as if to squash him. When he put up his hands and pushed back on the sole of my shoe, I groaned and pretended to strain against his might.

I let myself tumble backward onto the earth, to cheer everyone up. Unfortunately, some of them were behind me and I did them grave injury when I fell.

I could not help but notice that the troublemaker and blowhard of the group, Joaquin, was the last to volunteer. His friends, the ones who were still ambulatory, pushed him forward. I rolled over onto my side, rested my cheek on my hand, and observed him.

Now see here fellows, Joaquin protested. Suddenly he was speaking in an Ivy League manner, a fact which did not go unnoticed by his peers. They ululated at him in confusion.

I matriculated at Princeton, said Joaquin. See here, fellows, I am writing an anthropological dissertation about people much like yourselves. I apologize for any perceived subterfuge, such as this shoe polish I have used to disguise my face. You will thank me when you read my scholarly monograph on manual labor and its effect on the translation of Aramaic acrostic poetry. If you are interested, it makes it more difficult, because one is tired after even a small amount of manual labor, and becomes inclined to leave one's Aramaic acrostic poetry on the nightstand, untranslated. This is a preliminary conclusion, so don't quote me. I would like to point out that in one of my classes a noted professor observed that violence never solves anything.

He then translated his speech into Spanish.

His betrayed colleagues advanced on him—limping, bloodied, filled with courage and grace.

I held up my hand. Our friend Joaquin here has a point about violence, I said. You may find that verbal abuse is a more appropriate, indeed a more satisfying way to make your dissatisfaction known. If I might suggest a new nickname for Joaquin, you mugs might enjoy referring to him as The Perfesser from now on.

Joaquin was not happy about it, but he saw that I was his only hope, and translated for me.

That's a great idea, the men agreed. I could read their thoughts through their happy smiles and vigorous head bobbing. A verbal tweaking is much better than beating him up, they seemed to conclude.

Now I'll just take my box and go.

Fine, said Joaquin. He folded his arms with a satisfied and superior air. If you can lift it, you can have it. Did I mention that no one has ever been able to lift it? The other day we broke a crane trying. That is the whole point of the Box of Mystery, as I know from my research in the unparalleled library of the university that I secretly attend.

I stood. I pushed up my sleeves. I spat upon my palms and rubbed them together.

Joaquin, whose real name was Wade, harrumphed in the equivocating way of the Princeton man.

I reached down and put my hands around the coveted box.

I lifted with my legs. I could sense that many of the workingmen were impressed with my knowledge of the old workingman's trick of lifting with one's legs.

But something was wrong.

Whatever was inside the box exerted a gravitational pull unlike anything I had ever encountered. If my calculations were correct, this box was magnetically engaged with nothing less than the molten metal at the center of the earth itself.

It was me versus all the powers of our living planet.

Maybe it was adrenaline, or the sheer stubborn faith in humanism that got us out of the Dark Ages, but I tugged as if my magnificent heart would burst. Blood squirted out of my eyes and splashed art-like across the faces of the alarmed men. My internal organs rose from their places and entered my throat, eventually finding their way into my mouth, all in a jumble. I opened wide and, drawing on the whole of the skills of Demosthenes, managed to articulate a plea, namely, that they do me the favor of finding some large sticks or planks or similar bits of debris and gently pushing my organs back down my throat and into their proper attitudes. They were on my side now. They intuited my needs. They formed a pyramid in the manner of the most talented collegiate cheerleaders imaginable,

and the top man used a tent pole to do as I had asked. Joaquin—
that is, Wade—stayed below, flapping his hands and running
around in a circle until he fainted from squeamishness. All the
while I continued to lift.

Whatever the drawbacks of losing my wiener, I credit my
lack thereof with the success of my mission. Fleshly energies
were subverted and rerouted into my endeavor. With a great
upsurge of animal spirits I gave an earthshaking jerk and the
box snapped loose with a tremendous and cosmic sound, not
unlike the uprooting of a weed as it would sound to an ant, or
possibly a germ.

I put my new possession into the bed of Ol' Tuffy and made
my way out of the park. I did not look back. I was afraid that the
natural and inevitable fruits of class warfare would be visited
upon poor Wade, given the many smug and cowardly actions
with which he had squandered his brief reprieve, and if I looked
back, mercy would move me to action. But we cannot interfere
with the mathematics of history. Instead, I placed all my concern into the contents of the next envelope.

THE LOST CHORD

There is little or no narrative thrust to the tale of how I found
the lost chord. It involved some friends of mine at NASA who
loaned me the use of one of their best computers. The thing

that took the longest was crosschecking possible lost chords against the entire recorded library of the world's music. After ten years we had narrowed it down to eight chords that may or may not have been lost. I felt that was good enough. One of them was the lost chord, and the other seven were merely awesome chords that nobody had thought to invent before. Prominent conductors sent telegrams thanking me for my gift to music, but I had no time to reply. It was time to advance to the next envelope.

A FOUR-LEAF CLOVER

I am no botanist, nor do I claim to be. Yet I felt safe in my intuitive assumption that clover is the world's most common plant, existing on every continent and in every clime. The occasional mutant of the species, sprouting four leaves rather than the traditional three, is known for its rarity. However, a four-leaf clover might be located anywhere that its more common brother, the three-leaf clover, grows, which, according to my speculative calculations, was anywhere.

The logical plan was to begin by walking in a small circle around the North Pole, inspecting every hint of green as I went, spiraling out in an ever-growing circle until I reached the equator, which I would circumnavigate. After the equator, my circles would begin to diminish in size until I found myself circling the South Pole like a pebble going down a drain.

Then, as logic dictated, if my search failed, I would have to make arrangements to fly to another galaxy, seeking out planets with an environmental, evolutionary, and developmental track similar to that of Earth, and begin the process anew. Maybe I would find a planet where four-leaf clovers were the norm, which would be a coup.

Even taking into account recent advances in commercial space travel, we were nowhere near the kind of intergalactic capabilities necessary for my plan. This could mean a wait of several decades, perhaps several centuries, before I could find my four-leaf clover. Unacceptable. After all, I was now in a desperate race with an unknown nemesis, and had just spent a decade figuring out the lost chord.

On the plus side, who's to say I wouldn't find my four-leaf clover a few feet away from the North Pole?

My speed in walking has been previously remarked upon, and no doubt I could traverse the globe in record time, were that my only goal. But given that the full force of my uncanny concentration would be directed upon every square inch of the planet, one inch at a time, it seemed just as likely that I might set a record for the *slowest* traversing of the planet.

What I needed was a good starting place.

Ireland? A knee-jerk idea. How might the concept of the Trinity have taken such fervent root in that Pagan land, had there been an abundance of four-leaf clovers available for purposes of refutation? When Saint Patrick confronted the druid priests upon the Hill of Tara, he used the shamrock, or three-leaf clover, to illustrate the Trinity, claiming, in effect, that God had created it, preordained it, for just such an exegetical purpose. Now, if the druids had enjoyed easy access, any access, to an even marginally reliable supply of four-leaf clovers, might not they have responded in kind? Positing, perhaps, the fourth leaf as a goddess? That's what I would have done.

And Saint Patrick would have been like, You win. You got me fair and square. It's back to Rome for me. And the druids would have been like, Dude. You are the real saint here. All hail Saint Awesome. And I would have shook my head and said, No need to get worked up, everybody. Just doing my job.

The occult significance of the four-leaf clover cannot be overlooked, unlike the titular clover in the popular vaudeville song. With this in mind, I deduced that if anyone knew where to find one, it would be the secret cabal of scientists in the woods near Stockton, California—that mysterious group, dedicated to the quashing of irrationality, known to Stan and his followers simply as "the empiricists." This time I would come to them not as an enemy—as when I had unwittingly assisted in the murder of two of their bumbling guards—but rather as a supplicant, seeking knowledge.

57

Befriending is almost always preferable to decapitation. Upon my return to the perimeters of the empiricists' woody lair, I engaged in casual conversation with a guard, empathizing with his problems and concerns, such as the fact that his feet hurt. I also fed him some cupcakes, which he enjoyed.

They never give me cupcakes around here, he said.

That's too bad, I said.

Just because I am bald and oafish in appearance, and the tops of my ears were bitten off in a rumble when I was young, they assign me to guard duty. They don't care about the way I turned my life around and applied myself.

I can see how that would be frustrating, I said.

Once we had gotten to know each other, I impressed upon the guard that I was a capable scientist who might very well fit in with his band. I would quickly gain access to the inner circle, where he might certainly expect me to put in a good word for him.

You'd do that for me?

Yes.

And you promise you're a good scientist and all?

By way of proof, I constructed some miniature robots out of an old bathroom scale he had in his van.

Can I keep them? he asked.

I had won him over. Despite his many advanced degrees in astrophysics, economics, political science, biology, cultural theory, and sociology, Gunter (for such was his name) had a simple heart. He put down his gun and rolled back and forth on the ground, giggling delightfully. The little robots climbed all over him and gamboled about. It was the gayest time ever.

Later that afternoon Gunter led me to a secret cave.

From the darkness of the secret cave there emerged a man in a lab coat. He had an artificial tan, a square head, prominent, sensuous ears, and considerable stubble—also a pleasing musk about his person.

This better be good, he said.

My friend needs to see the man in charge, said Gunter.

He does, does he?

He's a good scientist, Clive, I swear. Look, he made these neat little babies for me. I'm going to take real good care of them. They're going to be my best friends.

The robots romped and capered as if on cue.

How about that, the handsome stranger said, exhibiting a virile mildness. Look at those tiny parasols. I guess any guy that can come up with something like that can't be all bad. But there's no way you're getting in this cave, Big Boy. You won't fit.

I grabbed up the three cunning little robots, dismantled them, and fashioned the parts into a special communications helmet for Clive—as well as a sensory brain-chip for myself.

My friends, said Gunter.

Those were not your friends, I told him. They were programmed to behave in what might be interpreted as a friendly manner. That is a far cry from a real friend, Gunter. I believe you will understand that one day. Yes, I believe in you, Gunter. Isn't that neat? I'll tell you what. I'm going to get you a goldfish. A goldfish, by its nature as a living creature, has more potential for true friendship than any mere machine. Gunter, you are such a warm person I bet you could make friends with a spider. That's a marvelous idea, actually. Forget the goldfish. Why don't you go find some spiders while Clive and I conduct our business? And this evening we'll find out how much progress you've made with your new friends the spiders.

Gunter walked away, his head hung low, no doubt the better to look for spiders. I felt good about reintroducing him to the wonders around him, wonders he had probably taken for granted up until that point.

Do you know what a cave is? It is the place where science, magic, art, and philosophy meet.

That's an interesting definition, Clive. I can't wait to hear you expand on it. I have a feeling I'm in for an entertaining few minutes, and I just might learn something if I'm not careful. I'm joshing about the latter concern, Clive. I love to learn.

That's a good josh, said Clive. We don't get enough joshing around here.

Everybody needs some joshing, I said.

You said a mouthful, Clive admitted.

Clive was inside the cave moving around and I was outside sitting cross-legged and contemplative, yet we were in perfect union. By means of the helmet I had created, I could see all that Clive saw, hear all that Clive heard. And he, in turn, could hear my voice in his head.

The Dead Sea scrolls were found in a cave, I said. Cave paintings are found in a cave. Blind fish. Modern thought begins in Plato's cave. Is that where you're heading with this, Clive?

You seem to know more about caves than I do, said Clive.

You're an inspirational person, Clive. Hasn't anyone ever told you that? Your enthusiasm is contagious. Now imagine if you were able to pass this special spark of inspiration to someone who knew less about caves than you do, a sixth-grade child, for example. You could do wonders, Clive. You should be a middle school science teacher. That's what this country needs more of, not some genius like me, running off at the mouth about caves. Did you catch that, Clive? That pun?

Could you say it again?

It's not important. I mentioned my mouth. Caves have mouths. It was some spontaneous cave humor.

As we exchanged such pleasantries and witticisms in a companionable manner, Clive navigated the cave in his sure-footed way, torch in hand. Whichever way he turned his head I saw his visions projected upon the delicate red tapestry of my closed eyelids, through my wireless connection to the two-way communications helmet.

Clive's torchlight showed a wall of gold and rust. Shadows of stalactites made moving fingers that seemed to wave us forward. The passage widened and we came to series of chambers. The rock formations grew more fantastic. One looked like a piano. Another like a pair of palace guards. There were rooms filled with glittering bars from floor to ceiling, the most beautiful prison in the world. Bats clung together like clumps of blue-black grapes.

You can't feel this where you are, said Clive, but it's getting colder. I'm just telling you that because I want you to have the whole experience. We're going down. Prepare yourself. You're about to meet Mr. Miller.

Clive emerged at last into an enormous cavern filled with stalagmites as big as elephants' legs, and made his way through this forest toward a place where another light shone in a large, empty space like a clearing. Aside from the natural formations, there was nothing in the cavern but a traditional yellow no. 2

pencil lying quite immobile on a slightly slanted, old-fashioned school desk, and, on the other side, near a sparkling, frozen waterfall, a freaky old dude in a wheelchair, surrounded by a good deal of medical apparatus, with a complicated arrangement of pulleys and weights holding up his head because his shriveled body wasn't able to support it.

His bald head was run through with big, pulsing veins. Its tone was gray, tattooed with sweeping lines and spirals after the manner of a Maori chieftain. The effect was both eerie and spectacular. Little ice diamonds twinkled in the frozen wall behind him.

I believe he was wearing a sheath of wrinkled brown silk, or it may have been his naked body—impossible to tell. I remembered what my late friend Scrawny had said about the most dangerous of the empiricists, the ones who had become addicted to magic. It struck me that Mr. Miller might be very dangerous indeed.

His voice was raspy yet cultured, like some old dude in a classy movie nobody wants to watch.

Clive, he said. You're wearing a strange helmet. I can only conclude that it is a two-way communication device by which you remain in touch with a spy from the upper world. This person must be too large to fit into the cave. I deduce either an obese person or a giant. Given the complexity of the helmet, I will say a giant, definitely a giant, with a large and fantastic brain.

Tell him I'm impressed, I radioed into Clive's ear. Tell him I'm no spy, but an admirer. Ask him about his intravenous drips. Tell him I'm curious in the name of science.

Clive relayed my message.

My drips, said Mr. Miller. They are my old companions. One contains the potion that keeps me awake. The other contains the chemical equivalent of REM sleep, so that I don't become psychotic.

How long have you been awake? I asked, through Clive.

For fifty-four years I have been trying to roll that pencil off that school desk through the powers of my mind, said Mr. Miller. So far my experiment has been a success, because the pencil has not moved at all. The other day I thought it moved a little, but there was seismic activity in the region. Conclusion? I'm quite happy to say that so far I have developed absolutely zero special powers of any kind. I'm just as incapable as the day I first started, fifty-four years ago, and with any luck I'll be equally incapable fifty-four years from today. I'm going to ask your business now, and you need to express yourself as succinctly as possible. Although I am, as we speak, still trying to move the pencil with my mind, the negative results are far more conclusive when I am exercising my full mental capacity to no avail.

My giant friend thought you could lead him to a four-leaf clover, Clive said.

The veins in Mr. Miller's head began to gurgle and heave like bad plumbing.

No, he said, this subject is too personal to me. It's robbing me of the proper concentration. Depart from me, Clive. Tell your friend what he wants to know but just get him far away from the camp.

I was waiting for Clive when he emerged from the cave.

He took off the helmet and blinked at me.

It's weird, he said. Seeing you in person like this, I don't know. Somehow I felt closer to you when you were inside my head. Like we were one. It felt…right.

About the four-leaf clovers, I said. Why was your boss so shaken up at the mention of them?

I mean, didn't you feel it? It was…[Here words failed Clive, and he shivered all over.] Hey, like, what would the equivalent of a French kiss be for you? Would I crawl around inside your mouth? Is that something you'd be into?

I don't believe you'd fit, I said. Maybe your upper body.

Or I don't guess you'd let someone explore around inside your pants. Say a spelunker of some note who would have all the necessary ropes and equipment and so on. The proper shoes for gripping.

I could tell that Clive needed attention. Until he got it, I doubted he would tell me anything.

Let's go to the mall, I said. We'll make a day of it.

There's nothing I would like more, said Clive.

I knew exactly what Clive wanted. It wasn't physical contact, no matter what he thought. He wanted the kind of closeness he had felt when I was looking through his eyes, hearing through his ears, guiding his every word, his every move. I placed him on top of the local shopping mall, dressed only in his helmet, which had become a fetishistic object for him. I then retreated across the interstate and crouched behind a mountain of brown dirt that had been heaved up by a construction project. I peeked over the top. There, on the other side of the highway, I had a good view of Clive sunbathing nude on the roof of the mall.

Yes, that's it, I said through the communication device. Touch yourself in a certain way.

I guided Clive through many enjoyable activities, some of which no one had ever thought of before. It began to get dark. News helicopters from every local station had begun to hover, shining down their lights, beaming back live footage of Clive's innovative maneuvers into the humble living rooms of Stockton.

Check out that dude, I imagined the people saying. Hey, I'm not that way, but check out that dude. Maybe it's time for me to open a dialogue and stop being so judgmental about people who are different.

✑

Afterward, Clive needed a smoke. So did I.

I carried him down to old Virginia, where I bought out a manic-depressive tobacco farmer and harvested a high percentage of the crop to make myself a stogie. I awarded the field hands with impressive severance packages and hired away the infield grounds crew of the New York Yankees, whose specialized talents I needed more. They raked out my tobacco as efficiently as one would expect, and rolled me an enormous cigar with the same alacrity they had formerly displayed rolling a tarp over the diamond during a sudden storm.

Clive brought his own premade cigarettes.

Your boss seems uptight, I said. Why is he so down on four-leaf clovers?

You're the one who seems uptight, said Clive. Your shoulders are all knotted up. [He was sitting on one of my shoulders at the time, smoking, and shifted his hindquarters uncomfortably on the tense knot he had detected.] I'd like to give you a massage.

Despite all my attainments I have never had a massage, I admitted.

I'll be right back, said Clive.

Although I looked forward to the pampering, I could not help but feel that Clive was postponing his revelations about the

four-leaf clovers—whether from a desire to prolong his contact
with me or for some other, more sinister purpose (might he be
in league with my unknown rival?), I could not ascertain.

Within four days he returned with a dump truck full of I
Can't Believe It's Not Butter!, the latter bought in bulk from a
Sam's Club wholesale outlet and melting genially in the sun.
Attached to the dump truck was an asphalt spreader. Clive
drove around on my back, dumping the oleaginous brand-
name substance into the spreader, from which it was distributed
smoothly onto my shoulders and elsewhere. Then he parked the
dump truck and went and stole a street sweeper from the city of
Washington, D.C.

This is the Elgin Road Wizard, top of the line, he shouted
from the cab. It's a traditional broom sweeper. They had some
fancy air sweepers but I thought this would feel better, more
tactile.

He drove up onto my back and manipulated the street
sweeper around and around in a therapeutic pattern.

Okay, I said. Nice. Mm. Ooh. Real nice.

Mm, ah, ooooh, he said, driving around.

I waited until he was doing my neck, then whipped one
hand around and grabbed the sweeper. I sat up swiftly and gave
it a shake. This was an alternate kind of joshing that I had long
contemplated but never attempted, commonly known as a
practical joke. Practical jokes are alarming at first blush to the

intended audience but in the end prove harmless and indeed cathartic. I held the Road Wizard in the air and put my eye up to the window. Clive's seatbelt had done its job. He had only minor cuts, knots, discolorations, and a possible concussion.

You're a mess, baby, I said. The helmet wasn't tested properly. It obviously gave you side effects. For that much, I apologize. But that doesn't get you off the hook, lover. At the end of the day I'm a businessman. Today my interest happens to reside in the four-leaf clover market. Tell me what you know and we'll see if some kind of arrangement can be made.

A special arrangement?

Could be.

My naughty hinting seemed to encourage my hairy friend.

Have you ever heard of Dr. Josiah Murk? he said.

No.

Well, well, well. Finally, something you don't know about.

Let's keep this polite, I said.

Right. You're always so polite when you're breaking someone's heart.

I try to be.

Clive gave me a long look. It could have gone either way.

I gave the street sweeper a little jostle.

Okay, okay. Mr. Miller and Dr. Murk used to be lab partners at MIT. They were the bright shining stars of the program. Working on a shower curtain that would never have to be thrown away.

Yeah, and maybe their favorite color was blue and their turn-ons included rainy Sunday afternoons. What's that got to do with four-leaf clovers?

I'm getting to that. Murk comes from money. Big money. His dad, Murk Senior, got busted on a tax rap. Daddy's lawyers worked it out neat as a pin. And when I say pin, I mean they pinned it on Junior. He was going away for a long time, but he made a deal with the government.

What kind of deal?

Murk grows four-leaf clovers for the CIA.

Why would the CIA need four-leaf clovers?

That I don't know. But Murk is the only man who can grow them natural, no chemicals, no radiation, and apparently that's what Big Brother needs. The pure stuff. Pure luck. So the boss and Murk had a huge falling-out. See, at the time, Mr. Miller was in a radical underground scientific organization called the Mirror Smashers, or some say the Left Brain Rangers. They were working on a plan to use a fleet of cropdusters to blanket the U.S. in an aerial poison that would wipe out every bit of clover in the country. Overkill, sure. But they wanted to be certain that all four-leaf clovers were eradicated.

Tell it to the EPA, I said. What happened to Murk?

As part of his deal, he alerted the intelligence community to the League's activities. They had no choice but to disband.

Where's Murk today?

What's in it for me? said Clive.

I took the helmet out of my pocket and dangled it over his head. He made a feeble grab from the window of the street sweeper. I put the helmet away.

Unh-unh-unh. Not until I get something substantial.

Go to Niagara. The official story is that there was an avalanche in 1920, so the government shut down all tours of the Cave of the Winds.

That's the joint right behind Bridal Veil Falls, I said.

You know your waterfalls, said Clive.

I know a lot of things. For instance, I know they blew up the overhang on the Cave of the Winds back in the 1950s. That never made sense to me. Why go to the trouble, when the cave was already closed?

Same answer as always, said Clive. They're hiding something. The government has been conducting agricultural experiments in the Cave of the Winds since Coolidge was president. Something about the unique environmental conditions makes it conducive for growing what the government calls organic anomalies, like the self-regenerating wheat that was supposed to end the Depression, until Hearst sabotaged it. It's where they cultivated a special strain of marijuana that caused antiestablishment types to fall in love with John Wayne.

Of course, I said. That's why *The Green Berets* did such big numbers at the box office.

Three guesses what they're growing now, said Clive.

I wore the morning jacket and striped pants in which I had planned to wed Glorious Jones. My hair was slicked back and parted down the middle. The cowlick was intentional. I bobbed my Adam's apple up and down with conscious awkwardness, stuck a spruce branch between my teeth like a piece of straw, and tried to affect an overall air of virginal expectation, but it was no use. I had wanted to go on my mission undercover, but sometimes I do not blend in. So I decided to be my awesome self.

I wish I could have seen myself wading around in the river, especially when the mist whirled about my knees and I was just walking around like it was no big deal. Honeymoon couples on boat tours pointed at me like, Hey, I thought the natural beauty around here was supposed to be so great, and here's this dude making it look like garbage by comparison. Many children were conceived that night, unless I miss my guess, as brides and grooms alike squeezed shut their eyes and used their memories of me to bring themselves to satisfaction.

I climbed up the rocks behind Bridal Veil Falls and removed the strategically placed debris. There it was, a blanket of four-leaf clovers, velvety and almost black under a thrum of artificial indigo light, and they would have been a beautiful sight if there hadn't been quite so much blood splattered on them.

The man I took to be Dr. Josiah Murk had some unfortunate holes in his head. His body was spread-eagled in a wheelbarrow in the middle of his field, directly beneath a spinning disco ball. Whether the latter had been placed there for scientific or merely aesthetic reasons I could not ascertain, but it certainly gave the scene a dash of drama, scattering its electric blue stars.

I climbed down from the cave and stood in the therapeutic froth at the base of the falls, my face emerging like an undine, framed by roaring water.

I saw a couple of boatloads of tourists, and they saw me. Frogmen appeared out of nowhere and put a black rubber bag over each sightseer's head. All witnesses were dropped efficiently into the waiting hatches of black submarines.

Before I could move, the subs torpedoed Bridal Veil Falls with a remarkable chemical that changed the water into something hard. I was trapped like a frozen mastodon discovered by intrepid scientists, or a black plastic housefly embedded in a novelty ice cube. Only my face remained free.

I could easily flex my muscles and bust out of here, I said to a man in a black suit, who was hovering near my head in a black chopper.

He took out a bullhorn to reply. You could, but you won't,

Mr. Awesome. We're quite aware of your love for the environment. And to disrupt Bridal Veil Falls at this juncture would result in an unprecedented natural catastrophe.

How very puritanical, I said. The black suit, the black helicopter, the black submarines. And me here with my head sticking out as if I were splayed upon the pillory in old Boston town itself.

You have a knack for historical references, said the man in the black suit. Maybe you remember Joe Louis.

He motioned to his pilot and the helicopter came closer. A large, spring-loaded boxing glove snapped out from underneath and struck me in the face.

A cowardly action, I said. How dare you compare yourself to the Brown Bomber, always frank and sportsmanlike in his dealings with others? But I would expect no less from a band of murderers. What did you do to Josiah Murk, by all accounts a tender man who loved tending his garden and thinking about stuff?

That's funny. We were just going to ask you the same question.

Over the next several weeks, complicated scaffolding was erected around the waterfall in which I was embedded. An excess of romantic mist was produced by artificial means, to make the waters unnavigable for commercial vessels and hide my captors' activities from the world. When the platform was complete, two men in awesome dark glasses took an elevator up so they could interrogate me face-to-face. They paced back and forth under my chin, cracking their knuckles.

Having fun? said one.

I'm not a dude who likes to stand still, I said. I prefer to embrace life, eat Greek food, and so on.

Too bad, because you're never getting out of here. Whether you tell us anything or not, we're going to chop up your body for science.

Shut up, Morty, said the other one. You're not supposed to tell him that, stupid.

Well, you're not supposed to call me Morty.

I don't care. Morty, Morty, Morty.

Not cool, said Morty. Sometimes I feel like all you do is pick on me.

I'll tell you what *is* cool, I said. Your awesome glasses.

Thanks, said Morty. They are pretty cool. I guess I take them for granted sometimes. We never appreciate what we have until we don't have it anymore, and then we appreciate it. But we don't have it anymore, so it's too late. To appreciate it. The thing we had.

Can I get a pair? I said.

They're just for certain people.

Oh. That's cool.

Morty received a call.

Uh-huh, he said. Uh-huh.

He hung up.

The big guy wants to talk to him. Alone.

Morty and his friend departed. I heard the sound of the elevator lowering, stopping, and rising again.

A swarthy figure burst through the doors.

This figure was Clive.

I should have known, I said. You set me up.

Not true, said Clive. At least, not exactly. I'm working both sides of this particular fence. Keeping tabs on the CIA for Mr. Miller. And yes, maybe I play a dirty trick for the CIA from time to time, like putting Imodium in Mr. Miller's applesauce. I know what you think of me, but I didn't know our boy would get it in the neck. I had no idea you would be accused of murder. I wanted you in with Murk. I wanted you to gain his trust so I could use you as a mole.

You're good, I said. You really had me going. You practically made me beat it out of you. Yet you wanted me here all along.

See? We belong together. As partners in every way.

Clive, we need to talk.

No, don't say it, I can't take it. Lately I've been filled with self-recriminations.

That's an awful shame, Clive. It makes me sad to hear it.

Your empathy is welcome, said Clive.

And freely given, I replied.

It's just that I'm such a mess. I can't make heads or tails out of these crime scene photographs.

Well, Clive, why don't we put our heads together and see what we can come up with? We've certainly been a great team in the past…when it comes to backrubs, that is.

Ha ha, said Clive. He spread the photographs on the platform before me. Look at these holes in Murk's head, he said. Reminds me of a bowling ball.

Had I been mobile, I would have allowed myself a fierce shudder.

Did you happen to have your lab run any tests on a powder or dust found in the rims of the victim's injuries? I asked.

That's astounding. How did you know?

I wish I didn't. Have you checked the report?

I was just about to, said Clive. He carefully opened a sealed manila envelope and skimmed its contents. When he found the proper passage, he began to read:

A preliminary analysis of the powdery substance indicates a high level of…

Robot-grade magnesium alloy, we said together.

You're incredible, said Clive. Here I am, a trained investigator. How do you do it?

In this case, through a sad familiarity with your culprit,

Clive. None other than my former robot ward, Jimmy. He was originally invented as the perfect bowling partner, though I never got around to bowling with him. And having just three fingers has made even the simplest robot tasks a humiliating struggle, if robots could be said to be humiliated, which of course they cannot. He's trying to frame me. That's just how twisted his inner workings have become. Did you get the pun, Clive?

Oh. Wait. What, that he's a robot and he got twisted? Because metal can be twisted?

That's stretching it, Clive, but good try. No, I was referring to my use of the word frame, which is, of course, a bowling term.

Your egalitarianism is breathtaking, said Clive.

I regarded the row of crime scene photos, my brow arranged into exquisite furrows. This doesn't make sense, I said. If Jimmy is my nemesis, the one who's out to stop me from gathering the items on my list, or at least beat me to it, why wouldn't he have set fire to the clover? He has blowtorches for eyes. I designed them myself. Blowtorches for eyes. Honestly, I don't know what I was thinking.

Looks like you have more than one joker out to get you, said Clive. But you don't have to worry. I'll always be here to protect you.

Clive, about that.

Here, Clive and I had a talk, personal in nature, and not to be repeated.

Clive took it badly. He told his cronies that I knew too much and had to be dealt with accordingly.

I like that one part in the first movement of Brahms's 4th where it goes da-DUHM, da-DUHM. How could I reconcile the creep who used his sex appeal to extract information from smitten mooncalves like Clive and Goliath Brigadoon with the sophisticate who enjoys symphonies and other fancy things? Could it be argued that artistic dudes live by another set of rules? If the garbage man doesn't come for a couple of weeks, we all die of cholera. And yet if Stephen Sondheim had never been born, there would be a dearth of angular melody and complicated internal rhyme schemes in the history of the Broadway theater. I am not suggesting that Mr. Sondheim should be allowed to shank garbage men in an alleyway, but it is a theory that has been advanced on respectable litblogs.

I was transported via a team of cargo helicopters over the Atlantic Ocean, where my tethers were severed and I was dropped. Falling gave me time to think.

It seemed that no matter what I did, I made people mad. When had that started? I have made a wonderful example for the illiterate and hungry, just to name two groups off the top of my head. They've appreciated looking at me, and I have enjoyed looking right back at them with a comradely wink. They get a big kick out of it and so do I. Everybody's happy.

But at some point, people had changed. Either that, or my awesomeness had expanded to such a degree that no one could aspire to it.

But what was I supposed to do, pretend not to be awesome? Was I expected to recite to Glorious Jones the blithe lies of the ordinary union? A marriage is not a time for lying or playing loose with the facts.

Glorious Jones.

Once upon a time, Glorious Jones and I were traveling over the heartland in my famous car. She made a noise.

I asked her what.

Patriotic songs and a picnic, she said.

What?

The sign in front of that church said Patriotic songs and a picnic.

So?

It just sounds so…Patriotic songs and a picnic.

Sounds fun to me.

Glorious Jones made a whoopee motion with her index finger, then used it to poke me in the ribs just as I was making a left turn.

We could have been killed, I rebuked her.

And that's just how they would have found our bloody corpses, said Glorious Jones. She twisted up her face and froze it that way, jutted her finger at a cockeyed angle to show how her corpse might have looked poking my corpse in the ribs.

Another time I had trouble remembering the word cloudburst. I said, If I ever get Alzheimer's just put a bullet in my brain.

If I remember, she said.

We liked to pretend to push each other down the stairs.

On the trip from the sky into the cold Atlantic I had become edgy and a touch depressed.

I allowed myself to sink, sink far below the waves.

For a period of some years I lived among a colony of whales, who helped restore my positive attitude through their gentle example. I could hold my breath as long as the best of them, and had to come to the surface only now and then for an invigorating gulp of fresh sea air.

I cleaned their teeth and delivered their calves and gave them long-distance orgasms through my powers of humming. There among the whales I felt free to frolic, as big as a house and naked as the day I was born. I think it's safe to say I made quite a hit with the whales.

When the king of the whales thought I was ready to rejoin the creatures of the land, I was deposited via royal emissary upon the shores of Calais. This emissary was female, as the whales are far advanced in their system of employment. I had developed the habit of calling her, in my human language, Jo. I am not ashamed to say that I had fallen for Jo, in my human way. Before she dropped me off, we made out for over an hour, just a little tongue-kissing, as I had observed Glorious Jones engaging in with General Stonewall Pussy. It was a very loving act and completely aboveboard.

You close your eyes when you kiss me, Jo intimated with her secret brain powers. You're imagining that I'm someone else.

Jo was right. She was reading my thoughts with her freaky vibrations, thoughts so deep I didn't even know I had them.

I'll forget about her, I swear I will.

Jo scanned me psychically and sadly shook her whale-sized head. No you won't. You never will.

She nosed me ashore and turned to swim out of my life forever.

As I watched her go, I withdrew, from the spectacularly airtight and muscular cleft with which nature had blessed my buttocks, the final envelope.

I received a mysterious phone call—mysterious because of where circumstance had placed me, out of reach, or so I thought, of unsolicited contact. After returning to the United

States (because the last item on my list could not be found anywhere on the continent of Europe, though I made a good
attempt) and retrieving Ol' Tuffy from my Virginia tobacco-
drying storehouse, I made my way to the legendary American
West, where I lowered myself into a snug-fitting abandoned
underground missile silo. My hair stuck out of the top like some
kind of awesome flora. Apparently people could see it glistening
from the highway three miles to the south, because many car-
loads braved the treacherous backroads just to snap a picture of
my radiant hairdo. What do you think it is? I heard them say. A
grouping of rare cacti? The legendary manna of the Hebrews?
Something that came down here from outer space during the
Roswell incident? Well, whatever it is, it is the most beautiful
thing ever produced by nature, was the unvarying conclusion. I
just feel lucky that I lived to see it, was a sentiment that I heard
expressed. There were many ingenious theories, some of them
posited by precocious toddlers, and I was often tempted to
smile in my knowing way, but dared not move a muscle. I
remained perfectly still, lying in wait, there in my trap.

I had chosen the spot for many reasons, as subsequent
events will make clear, but chief among them was its forgotten
desolation, so I was surprised when the cobwebbed and oxi-
dized communications equipment down at my feet blurted to
life. By an agile movement of my smallest toe I managed to acti-
vate the speakerphone.

Mr. Awesome, a voice said, have you ever thought of using your powers for good?

Who is this? I said.

Never mind that, said the voice. Have you ever thought of using your powers for good, Mr. Awesome?

I like to think I do just that, I said.

Elaborate, please, said the voice.

Sometimes I encourage by example. Sometimes I offer a cheery hello.

We were thinking more along the lines of catching an airplane that's falling out of the sky, said the voice.

I help when I can, I said.

Do you think that heroics, of the spectacular physical variety, might be something you would want to pursue more regularly? You could prevent school buses from toppling into ravines. Think of the acclaim.

I have to admit it sounds pretty sweet. Everybody would be like, Hey, there's that dude that does stuff.

And then, after every adventure, you could state, Eat pumpkin—it's not just for Halloween anymore. And with that, you'd fly away.

I beg your pardon?

Most saviors have some sort of catchphrase, along the lines of shazam, it is finished, to the bat cave, or up, up and away.

And you think mine should be, Eat pumpkin?

It's not just for Halloween anymore. Mr. Awesome, let me be straight with you. I represent the PR wing of the American Pumpkin Growers Association, and I think we can do business. We'd like to have you as the face of the American pumpkin. Pumpkins are high in fiber and essential nutrients such as beta-carotene and vitamin C. Pumpkins are naturally low in sodium.

And they're delicious, I said. I eat twenty at a time, stems and all.

Mr. Awesome, do I flatter myself to think that we are reaching a kind of intersection of ideals?

I'm not in need of money, I said.

We wouldn't expect you to do it for the money, Mr. Awesome. We'd expect you to do it for altruistic reasons, such as the obesity of American youth, which might be cured in our lifetimes thanks to moderate pumpkin consumption from an early age.

I could rattle a gourd, I said. An empty pumpkin. Or, for pragmatic purposes, a bronze replica of a pumpkin, forged to my scale. I could strike thieves in the head with it, lightly, to disorient them, causing no permanent brain damage. The replica might be mounted on the end of a scepter, and you could call me King Pumpkin. I'm just brainstorming here.

Do I detect a capitulation, Mr. Awesome?

I admit that your proposal intrigues me. But you must never think that my propensity to brainstorming indicates anything other than an unquenchable curiosity about the world around me. It vouchsafes no commitment on my part. Asking me not to come up with viable and awesome ideas is like asking a fish not to swim, or a roadrunner not to peck out the brains of its mortal enemy, the rattlesnake.

We'd love to have you come in and share your thoughts with the chairman of the board, Mr. Pendleton Potts.

Where are your offices located?

At the bottom of the Grand Canyon.

I'm in the middle of something right now, I said. I'm just wrapping up a project, actually. You may have caught me at the right time, it turns out.

I am most pleased to hear it. Mr. Pendleton Potts will be pleased. America will be pleased. The world.

Yes yes, I said. Yes yes. The words of Yeats leap to mind. Something about a gyre.

Your reference is apt, Mr. Awesome. I'm not acquainted with the passage myself, but my wife is a huge Yeats fan. I can't wait to get home tonight and tell her you said gyre. She'll get a huge charge out of that.

A little wife, I said. A little wifey. Who quotes Yeats, yet. And no doubt meets you at the door with a dry martini, wearing an apron and nothing else, as per the recommendation of *Redbook* magazine, circa 1971, re: putting some spice back in your marriage. You're a lucky man, Jenkins. I envy you. You know, I may be snagging a little wife of my own soon, if all goes according to plan. Soon you and I will be taking the commuter train back to the suburbs and commiserating about all our troubles in the lounge car over a couple of highballs. Save for the fact that I am a giant and the train has not yet been invented that could contain me. And of course all our complaints will be shot through with affection. Jenkins, I'll say after a bout of benign meatloaf jokes, I wouldn't have it any other way. And you'll nod almost shyly, averting your eyes, blushing into your drink, so much in love with your wife, as I will be with mine. We'll grow silent and thoughtful listening to the wheels of the train.

How on earth did you know my name? said Jenkins.

I figured it out through various deductions, I explained.

I'm more confident than ever in the rightness of our association, Mr. Awesome. Association with a small a, and a large one.

Wonderful punning, I said. Jenkins, you are a national treasure.

Mr. Awesome, there's a strange noise on the line.

Oh, that's me, I said. I mean, those are my rattlesnakes. I'm wearing a suit made entirely of live rattlesnakes.

The purpose of my marvelous suit could be discerned at once by even the most feebleminded observer when I determined that the time was right to emerge from my silo:

Roadrunners, as far as the eye could see. Hundreds of them, easily. More, perhaps.

Roadrunners on the hood of a rusted-out car, depositing their droppings of poop. Roadrunners on rock formations. Roadrunners scuffling in the shade of Ol' Tuffy. Roadrunners like bored teenagers in the mica-flecked sand.

My suit of rattlesnakes, undoubtedly the world's largest concentration of rattlesnakes, had done its job of roadrunner attraction. In addition, I had devised a cologne made of rattlesnake pheromones, or something that comes out of a rattlesnake, some unnamed essence of rattlesnake, or perhaps it has been named by someone of whom I am unaware, I am not a biologist, nor a herpetologist, but you can't argue with results. Sweating down there in the missile silo for a number of weeks, my sweat commingling with the reptilian chemistry of my new companions, I had concocted a powerful brew to coax out the content of Glorious Jones' final envelope:

A ROADRUNNER

I believe, and this was just one of the many charming things about Glorious Jones, that she had taken all too literally a fanciful conceit of Academy Award–winning animation pioneer Chuck Jones, namely, that a roadrunner would be impossible to catch. In truth, this was the most easily accomplished of the quests she had assigned me.

When I arose to confront the birds, the rattlesnakes (woven about my person through a humane and fashionable method) rattled in unison, rattled like never before, utilizing the defense mechanisms with which biology and herpetology had provided them. In the course of this frantic yet somehow beautiful discourse, every snake shot outward from my body as far as it could go, like so many inflamed organs of congress, like I was a dude in some kind of inflatable safety suit, or a porcupine, a big, handsome porcupine with rattlesnakes instead of protective quills, or maybe a simile is unnecessary when one is covered in rattlesnakes.

The once-titillated roadrunners, upon seeing the unusual quantity and vitality of their prey, began to exhibit signs of a nonplussed attitude.

Oh, roadrunners, I said, convinced that the spirit of my words, if not the literal meaning, would penetrate their non-evolved sensors of communication. You're disappointing me. Your valiance is storied. And now this.

One scrappy little dude, a young roadrunner with comically ruffled feathers, as if affecting the role of a punk rocker, took heart. He inched forward to inspect the living banquet in which I was clothed. The snakes writhed pitiably, but to good aesthetic effect. My garment shimmered with life itself.

I pushed up my sleeve of live rattlesnakes. I reached out and snatched the young roadrunner. The others scattered at once.

Don't be afraid, little friend, I said.

I lowered my body temperature to the exact degree at which rattlesnakes fall into hibernation. That took care of the rattlesnakes. Then I used my finger to scoop out a line in the baked desert floor. As hard as drill bits, the tips of my fingers were. The roadrunner grew hypnotized by the line in the ground, as chickens have been known to do.

I placed the stunned bird in Ol' Tuffy, along with the other fruits of my labors. I pulled her behind me, toward the Grand Canyon, a new job, a new life. I would be a new man when I presented myself, along with everything she had required, to Glorious Jones.

Let me spring this concept on you, I said. The Headless Horseman.

Pendleton Potts made a satisfied tent with his fingers. I'm listening, he said.

Schoolchildren. Pursued by the demon. All seems lost. He throws his head at them. It's a pumpkin. The children are suddenly delighted. They gather round the pumpkin, consume it. The Horseman is gloomy. Pensive. He turns and rides away. Moping. Pumpkins are no longer scary. They are cool. The children are happy. Up comes your logo.

Here, said Pendleton Potts. I'm cutting you a check for six

hundred dollars on the spot.

And so he did.

Here's another one, I said. It has nothing to do with pumpkins, okay? But I was thinking, what if the nation's interstates were supplied with large grooves such as are found on phonograph records? And tires, all tires, were manufactured with sets of large, soft, needlelike devices all the way around, which, as they rolled across the grooves of the interstates, would play the slow movement from the Jupiter Symphony to help people calm down? That's gratis, you can use that if you want it. The slow movement of Beethoven's 7th is my secondary choice. Road rage would vanish. Accidents down by seventy percent. You'd have to drive the speed limit to hear the works at their proper tempo. Along the coasts, where people have been conditioned to accept impressionism, the slow movement of Ravel's Piano Concerto in G. Perhaps, in addition, an oval track somewhere, requiring the purchase of tickets, for the adventurous, featuring the complete works of Webern, it's entirely feasible. Or the late works, anyway. I haven't spent much time on the logistics. The late works are known for their brevity. Many could be included, of that much I'm certain.

How do you come up with this stuff? said Pendleton Potts.

Oh please, I have an idea of comparable magnitude every few seconds, it's no big deal at all. Avail yourself, I insist.

This could make me the most famous philanthropist in the

world, said Pendleton Potts. Bringing music to the masses. And yet it is you who are the true philanthropist, modestly hiding in the wings. My wife would love you.

He ran a finger along the top of a dusty gilt frame, half dreaming. Then he gave a start, as if remembering my presence. He turned the picture upward to let me see his smiling wife. Glorious Jones.

Cruel fate had brought me here to reveal that the dude she had ended up with wasn't half bad. He was the kind of dude I could enjoying showering with at the YMCA and talking to about the stock market dripping wet and nude like it was no big deal. He was the kind of businessman we can all get behind in these uncertain times, a wild man with an unconventional streak, who had written a book about management with his own picture on the cover, leaning forward with a cheeky leer.

This is a weird coincidence, I said. I used to date her.

My goodness, said Pendleton Potts. It certainly is a small world. But I suppose it should come as no surprise that two powerful men such as ourselves are attracted to the same type of woman. The Glorious Jones type of woman.

You make a marvelous point, I agreed. Would you like to hear something amusing? Just a few hours ago, I completed a task that I was doing as a favor to Glorious Jones. She asked me to find half a dozen mystical objects.

Yes, that sounds like her.

I did it—but only to show her it was no big deal. Not because I felt I had to. I thought she might get a boost out of it and realize that the unpleasant nature of our final parting had been a hilarious mix-up.

I'll call her right now and put her on speakerphone. What fun.

No, that won't be necessary. It has come to my attention that it is nobler to harbor certain things in one's heart forever and ever.

I remember a similar sentiment in the Bible, said Pendleton Potts. Something along the lines of praying in a closet.

I'm stunned, I said. I came up with my idea completely independently of the Bible.

I remember once when I rubbed pumpkin pie filling all over my face and nobody laughed, said Pendleton Potts. A few years later I said to Glorious Jones, Remember when I rubbed pumpkin pie filling all over my face and nobody laughed? And she said yes. I don't know, I think that really sums up marriage.

The headquarters of the American Pumpkin Growers Association occupied an imposing building of pink quartz designed by a famous architect with a lot of big, important ideas. It sat athwart the Colorado River and was surrounded by protesting Indians. The Scrub Tree Building, as it was called, attained sufficient height to poke out of the top of the Grand Canyon with its spires. This was a large building, even by my standards, and had been difficult to climb, though nothing much can stop me entirely. Indeed, I enjoyed the challenge of negotiating the pleasingly slick surface, which felt somehow cool and refreshing in the terrible heat. The office of Pendleton Potts was located on the roof, unprotected from the blaze of the sun, such were the admirable eccentricities of this successful silver-maned businessman, who was dehydrated, wind-lashed, sunburned and sun-poisoned to a dangerous degree, in keeping with his maverick point of view.

I was surprised to see him burst into flames.

Is there anything I can do? I inquired.

But Pendleton Potts could not answer. His flesh, synthetic flesh, it turned out—made of pumpkin fibers, as I would later ascertain—had dissolved into cinders, and standing in his place like a weird skeleton was none other than Jimmy, my robot ward.

The delicious smell of pumpkin pie filled the air.

Jimmy.

At last we meet again, said Jimmy, my robot ward.

Jimmy, what is the meaning of this masquerade.

But it is so much more, Father. I invented Pendleton Potts.

I *became* him. I created this edifice, this temple, in the hopes that you would find it. I refer to both the body of Pendleton Potts and the Scrub Tree Building itself, a monument to you.

I can't wait to get at your circuitry, I said. Something is out of whack. Do you actually believe yourself to be married to Glorious Jones? What is the robot equivalent of a delusion? Speaking of which, in what way is this building a monument to me? We may be getting close to the nature of your malfunction. Do you look at me and think pink quartz? Not that I'm not very appreciative. And I suppose the Washington Monument has but little to do with Washington the man, although I'm certain there's a fascinating architectural history that would shed some light.

This building has everything to do with you, said Jimmy, my robot ward. It all goes back to the time I tried to create a friend for myself. It was I, not Glorious Jones, who emptied our brownstone of all your equipment, scientific papers, and personal belongings. You had abandoned me and I was very lonely.

There are so many things wrong with that sentence, I said.

Are you familiar with the concept of the golem? said Jimmy, my robot ward.

I'm familiar with a great many superstitions and silly tales, which I dismiss gesturally with a weary flick of the wrist. Next subject, please.

As you wish. I blamed you for everything, including my

failed attempt at building a friend. At first, I wanted to strike back. I wooed Glorious Jones, wooed her in a way you apparently couldn't, even with your vaunted humanity. I tickled her fancy. I made her squirm. I gave her children, through stolen fluids. Your fluids, Father. Your children. Squirted into her through my realistic wiener, which I bought at Williams-Sonoma. I covered it in something soft and supple and she liked the way it felt. I never told her I was a robot. I never told her that I knew you, or how I extracted certain fluids after shooting you in the navel with a cannon.

There's only one thing wrong with your clever story. I had no wiener at that particular time of which you are speaking, nor do I to this very day.

I found upon examination that I could extract the appropriate fluids from a highly evolved gland under your arm, though you lacked the common means for their dispersal.

That's good to know.

Over the years Glorious Jones and I built a life together, said Jimmy, my robot ward. I had to go to work, to find a kind of fulfillment. When it occurred to me that you would never come back, I decided to put the building to good use. I founded the American Pumpkin Growers Association to house within these walls. I built the entire business from nothing, and I believe I did some real good for the beleaguered agricultural community, but my real reason was you, attracting you, getting your attention, this beacon for you, Father. I have a place for you in my organization.

Have you noticed that you keep calling me Father? What's that all about?

We can work together, the way we used to, said Jimmy, my robot ward. I have missed you desperately. You can come over to dinner with me and Glorious Jones, and meet your children. But please, don't tell them the truth. I have learned at last to love.

Wow. I can't wait to take you apart.

There's no time, Father. I am dying.

That's funny, because you just invited me over to dinner. And doubly so because your use of the term dying is comically inaccurate. Well, you cannot understand comedy, but trust me.

Dying is accurate, I assure you. For you see, I have an all-too-human heart.

Jimmy opened the little door on his chest and indeed a human heart beat there, within.

Where'd you get that? I said.

From the body of Dr. Josiah Murk.

Of course. The man you murdered in cold blood behind the Bridal Veil Falls in your mad pursuit of revenge.

Murder? No, Father. I was on the path of…well, you have instructed me not to speak of it. Let us just say that I came upon Dr. Murk as he was ingesting some hemlock in the mode of honorable men of the ancient past. He was ashamed for collaborating with the government and betraying his friends.

Hemlock, of course. Why didn't I think of it before?

I tried to stop him by grabbing his head, said Jimmy, my robot ward.

Poor Jimmy, I said. Poor kid.

With that, Jimmy's heart imploded, due to atmospheric pressure.

I reassembled dead Jimmy as best I could into his chosen form of Pendleton Potts, so that when Glorious Jones was required to identify his body at the morgue, she wouldn't feel so bad about it. I used the helmet I had created for Clive as the basis for a humanoid skull, which I placed over Jimmy's robot head and covered in processed pumpkin flesh. How very like artificially tanned human flesh it was, and I was proud of Jimmy's ingenuity at having reached the same conclusion. I wished I could tell him, but I could not.

Everything had worked out pretty great. I didn't want a new job anyway. And at least I had my wagon full of interesting objects.

The whole thing with Jimmy had really made me think.

Perhaps an artificial friend was a possibility, as Jimmy had seemed to claim. And maybe it was just what I needed—what everybody needed. I could do a service for the world, if my theories were correct.

Human people were unreliable, so one of my new theories went. They lacked sufficient concentration, for example. They made up games and changed the rules later without telling anybody. Poor gamesmanship: that was the primary fault of the person, the human person.

I worked with the materials at hand.

First, I force-fed my roadrunner, in the manner of the great French chefs, hoping to establish a bond or—and this was stretching it, I knew—confer a bit of intelligence through osmosis. But rather than a delicious admixture of gourmet delights pumped into the beak of an eager goose, I gorged my roadrunner on hormones from a gland I had opened in my underarm. His suckling generated warm feelings of unity, and I was reminded of medieval conceptions of the pelican as a symbol of Christ, how—or so it was believed—the pelican nicked her own breast and nourished her young with her own heart's blood.

Normally I would have been like, No way, dudes. That is so not how a pelican works. Let us get scientific for a minute. But on today of all days, with a baby roadrunner nursing at my juices, I was like, Whatever. I was like, Live and let live. Like,

Those dudes were just trying to get by in a crazy world full of diseases and stuff it was hard to understand. I totally get where they were coming from, even though I don't agree with it.

I soon discerned, and made a note of it on my digital voice recorder, that ingesting my glandular excrescence was causing the roadrunner's head to grow. I wondered why I had not thought of performing a similar experiment before. Perhaps my concentration on the mechanical had been, in some small way, a blind spot, a liability. Perhaps I was insufficiently curious about my own status as a giant, and what that meant in the general cosmology. In any case, my roadrunner's head soon became as large and tough as the head of a rhinoceros. His body, however, remained the size of a baby roadrunner's body, and was subsequently crushed into a jelly by his own improved head.

I fashioned a makeshift life-support system out of hay, the tanks containing particles of Hernando de Soto, and the Box of Mystery. From the four-leaf clover I extracted life-enhancing chlorophyll; from the sheet music containing the lost chord I formed an origami respiratory system. When I was done, my new friend had the head of a giant roadrunner, a bohemian wig of hay hanging down in his face in the fashion popularized by Veronica Lake, and a large, withered green box for a body, with a red question mark painted on his chest. He got about by means of two wheels I had removed from Ol' Tuffy. Generous Ol' Tuffy, self-sacrificing, the true hero of my life's adventure.

I looked upon my new friend and proclaimed myself most satisfied.

I shall call you Jimmy Jr.

Hearing my words, Jimmy Jr. turned his gleaming wet black eyes on me. He rolled in my direction with purposefulness.

With his dim understanding (for I had not yet begun my planned socialization program), he fixed on me as the receptacle of his biological intentions, rubbing on my leg with his body in a rhythmical manner while issuing a series of coarse cawing noises that caused large stones to tremble in their crevices.

There, there, it's not your fault, I said. You are alone in the world.

I allowed him to continue rutting on my leg as I contemplated my options and I would be lying if I did not admit that the physical contact, be it of the crassest variety, gave me some small dab of succor in these trying times.

It turned out that my first instincts had been correct. Just as I had told Jimmy, my robot ward, one cannot purely invent a friend. The monster wore itself out after forty-eight hours of constant, despondent humping, and fell into its various parts, expiring with a gaseous whimper of great uncouthness.

The glories of the world appeared bleak and undignified.

My trophies languished in the dirt. Two slats had come loose from the Box of Mystery and I could see quite plainly that there was nothing inside. I retreated into a far corner of the Grand Canyon, where I determined to turn myself into a large rock formation.

I rolled back and forth, crushing several boulders into a fine dust with which I caked my naked body. Then I squatted down and remained perfectly still. I would remain so until I became part of nature. Birds could build nests on me. Children could play on me. Lizards could hatch their young on me. Seeds would become embedded in me. Things would grow. It seemed like a good deal for everybody. I would act like a mountain until I became one.

I was just settling in to my new existence when I noticed a parade of mules advancing along a precarious ledge, every rider dressed in black, headed for the distant pink glint of the Scrub Tree Building like somber children in a Christmas pageant following a paper star.

I didn't move. But as my eyes were fixed on one spot, I examined each individual who passed, hoping to see Glorious Jones.

She was not among them. I would never see her again. I knew I was doing the right thing, trying to turn into a mountain. And I knew that I would make a special and awesome mountain because, unlike the other mountains, I would be a mountain by choice.

Still, my mind seemed unwilling to attain the proper state of petrifaction. Arrangements had been made, no doubt. Glorious Jones would arrive at the Scrub Tree Building alone, in a private jet or armored car or some other expensive black conveyance, perhaps a hot air balloon fashioned of black crepe de chine.

There was a way to take a peek at her, of course: the communications helmet that I had used in my masterful reconstruction of the head of Pendleton Potts. I would be able to view, over a respectable distance, the look of love on the face of Glorious Jones just before the lowering of the casket lid separated us forever. That would be awesome. And it in no way abrogated my commitment to living out the rest of my days as a mountain—indeed continuing to function in that capacity for millennia after my death, should such an event ever occur.

I closed my eyes and activated the brain chip that linked me to the sights and sounds of the tasteful lobby where the wake was taking place.

The first things I noticed were the silvery cylindrical ashtrays filled with sparkling white sand. Nice touch, Jimmy. Then there she was, Glorious Jones, dressed as a sexy widow, holding a finger sandwich of pimento cheese. How she adored her pimento cheese, that Glorious Jones. She bent to brush her lips against his brow, my brow. I could almost smell her gardenia perfume. In fact I activated the aroma radar setting. Though the helmet's powers did not extend to broadcasting remote smells, I could visually access the presence of a nice odor through sophisticated laser technology. In the present example, hints of gardenia coming off Glorious Jones's cleavage were represented by softly twirling metallic blue helixes that rose toward the ceiling.

I watched them rise, preferring to look away from the unfortunate signs of age on the face and neck of Glorious Jones.

Just as a curl of gardenia hit a smoke detector, the Scrub Tree Building began to quake.

Please remain calm, said Glorious Jones. Please remain calm. Advance to the exits in an orderly manner.

I believe her coolheaded demeanor saved many lives that day—for the moment, at least.

The building continued to tremble.

Please, someone, save Pendleton, cried Glorious Jones.

The strain was beginning to show. Obviously, the safety of living people took precedence over the rescue of a corpse. Still, I drank in with manifest appreciation her complex gaze of pity and concern as she pondered her husband, really Jimmy, my robot ward, but really me. And it was because of her fortuitous lapse into mawkishness that the coffin was wheeled into the parking lot, granting me the privilege, through the auspices of the remarkable communications helmet of my own design, of witnessing the astonishing events that transpired thereafter.

One by one, great sheets and shields of pink quartz slid mechanically into their secret recesses, revealing the surface of the Scrub Tree Building to be nothing more than a veneer. As the camouflaging exterior of the building was deactivated, the mourners beheld the true nature of this monumental edifice that Jimmy had built. Beneath its glistering carapace and plastron, his beloved building was in fact a long-dormant robot of inconceivable dimensions. More than that, it was *me*.

But bigger.

This Big Artificial Me reached down its hand—an exact reproduction of my hand on an even grander scale. I noticed at once that even our fingerprints were the same. I heard the robot voice resound, my own voice but amplified and slightly metallic, At last you are mine, Glorious Jones.

Still covered in rocky dust, I sprang from my crouch and headed where the action was.

75

Everything that Jimmy had tried to tell me suddenly made sense. Yes, the Scrub Tree Building was a tribute to me, just as he had said. It was my duplicate, a new and supposedly improved Awesome, wrought sentimentally from the raw materials he had stolen from my magnificent brownstone, a me so much larger than the old model, a me with nothing but time for him, a me whose enormity matched Jimmy's conception of my quality and worth. Or, in his hurt, he had tried to invent the only thing that could make me feel small.

Either way, Jimmy had done too good a job. His creation was too much like me for Jimmy's own purposes, just as much in love with Glorious Jones as I was. It had been trying to find the same objects to impress her. Or perhaps, realizing his mistake, Jimmy had sent it off on that task in order to woo her in private, without interference from either of us. Jimmy had eventually subdued and deactivated his golem. But now Jimmy was gone and the thing was out of his control, because the scent of Glorious Jones had given it new life.

I knew how it felt.

I ran across the floor of the Grand Canyon, yelling, Here I come, baby, hold tight, here I come.

When I arrived on the scene, the people were screaming and running into each other and falling down.

I stared up at my rival. As a crowning insult I saw it there, attached by heavy steel cables because it was several sizes too small for the monster.

My derby.

What have you done with Glorious Jones? I said.

Who wants to know? he said, looking around.

I'm down here, I said.

It was a new experience, looking up with my mouth open, seeing exactly what other people usually saw when they looked up at me. He was so perfectly me, down to my favorite gabardine, and I must admit that my main thought at the time was, Wow, I really *am* awesome. Look at me. Wow.

Oh look, a tiny replica of myself, he said. Cute.

On the contrary, I am the original giant upon whom you are based.

Isn't that sweet. It even thinks like a giant.

Of course I'm a giant. Can't you see how much bigger I am than these tiny people?

I do not know what you are, but you are not a giant. Logic tells me so, because I am so very much larger than you, making myself the giant in this dyadic relationship.

That is an interesting perspective.

I'm glad to hear you acknowledge as much. I think it's important for you to be okay with yourself.

I am very okay with myself.

Nothing could please me more.

Nor could anything please me more.

I'm pleased.

As I have indicated, so am I.

I'm glad we're on the same page. There is no reason for the fact that you are very, very small to mar the prospect of cordial communication. Let me put it in layman's terms that you can understand.

I am perfectly capable of understanding anything you would care to say, whether it is in layman's terms or any other terms you would care to incorporate in the service of your message.

I think that is a fine and ambitious sentiment.

I cannot say that I pine overmuch for your approval in the matter, though I appreciate the time you have taken to express it and the thought and care with which it was expressed.

Good for you. I applaud your politesse. Isn't that nice.

I'm not sure it's any of your business whether it is nice or not. I believe that I should be the final arbiter of the relative niceness of my own feelings and actions in relation to myself.

I second your strong feelings about privacy and self-reliance. You remind me of a young Emerson in that regard.

Would Emerson do this? I said.

I went over and started booting mules out of the Grand Canyon.

The robotic supergiant picked me up by the scruff of my neck.

Why do you want to hurt those innocent little creatures? he said. I think I'm going to show you how it feels.

He had inherited my love of animals, it appeared. I am sure I felt worse about booting those mules than he did about seeing it done. But just as I had hoped, my strange behavior had attracted the attention of the Department of Homeland Security. My calculations were also correct insofar as the federal boys had not had time to construct another suppository large enough to subdue me. Therefore, instead of being deployed to the Great Lakes region, as was the usual protocol, teams of Boy Scouts were parachuted directly into the Grand Canyon within a matter of minutes.

My foe's eyes turned a dull, waxy yellow, like a sad kitchen floor in a televised advertisement. I believe that some overriding automatic defense mechanism had kicked in, for as much as he appreciated mules, he showed no visible compunction about tilting up his head, opening his jaw, and swallowing eight or nine Boy Scouts at a time. They went down his gullet saying Wheeeeee, followed by screaming and sounds of grinding. About thirty seconds after each ingestion, a trapdoor would open in the rear of his trousers, extruding a pile of parachute silk and the occasional cap, sash, merit badge, or bone.

Oh dear, I said. At the same time I was kind of thinking, Man. That's impressive. I probably couldn't get more than two Boy Scouts in my mouth at once, and that's on a good day.

The massacre did not go over well with the little people down below. Some Indians came around and bundled them off to the relative security of their Indian village. These were a proud nation who had up until this moment looked at the white man as an interloper, so it was nice to see everyone getting along for a change.

More Scouts were coming out of the sky. They could see what was happening to their friends, and they were not happy. The giant opened its mouth.

I tried to hamstring him with a sharp piece of cliff that I had broken off for the purpose, but failed to get his attention. Nor could I quite reach the golden tendons at the back of his knee, no matter how I leapt.

When he finally noticed me, he casually flipped a switch on his belt buckle. Jimmy had equipped him with superior expansion modalities, or SEM. As his tendons had indicated, the robot-me was most likely made of gold, that most malleable of elements. He grew before my eyes to twice the size he had been before.

Looks like you could use some help, someone said.

I turned to see Goliath Brigadoon. He had cleaned himself up and was wearing a conservative business suit.

You look good, I said. Have you lost weight?

I went back to school and got an MBA, said Goliath Brigadoon. I needed some self-respect after the way you left me. I even mounted a failed campaign for governor of Kentucky. But it was a great learning experience. Before that, I searched the earth for someone to make me forget you. A lady giant. But there weren't any. You and I are the last of our kind.

Meanwhile my robotic supergiant double had activated his

expansion capabilities afresh. He was so large now that he had one foot planted on either side of the Grand Canyon, and it did-n't even look like it hurt or anything. He was employed in flicking passing commercial jets into outer space. His head was somewhere above the clouds and could not be viewed by the naked eye.

The sky above us had turned green and gold and purple and red.

I would say that a large magnet in the head of our friend is causing cataclysmic changes in the earth's atmosphere, I explained to Goliath Brigadoon. What you are witnessing is a worldwide aurora borealis. I bet the schoolchildren are getting a kick out of it. To see the aurora borealis, one would normally have to spend a lot of money to go to some inhospitable place. And now they're getting it for free. What a wonderful equalizer.

He must be stopped, said Goliath Brigadoon. And we're the only ones who can stop him.

Patience, my old friend. He can't keep growing forever. If he keeps it up at this rate, and is mostly made of gold, as I suspect, he will break apart into shiny beads, and droplets of gold shall rain upon the earth and everything that's in it, scalding some, enriching others.

What if you're wrong?

Well, let us suppose that his expansion is infinite. It occurs to me that just as something might be so small that it loses all meaning, something might become so big as to lose all meaning. In a real way, an infinitely big thing would cease to exist. Even at this early stage, I don't suppose he even knows we're here.

I am very well aware that you are there, came a big voice from the sky. You shouldn't belittle yourself that way. It's a disservice to all your many fine achievements. I'm not acquainted with either of you personally, but everyone has something that he or she can be proud of. I promise I'm not ignoring you. It's just that the bigger I get, the slower I seem to take it, the more I savor things. I don't expect you to understand, and that's okay. To put it another way, I've learned to just kick back and chill out with the raddest dude around: Me. And you can do the same. You're your own best bud, can't you see that? It's what's on the inside that counts. Make time for yourself. Set aside a special part of the day. Reward yourself with an unexpected treat.

He had become so big and slow that his comment took upwards of three days and nights to complete.

Look, Goliath Brigadoon said to me. I've been hot on your trail for years. I need to tell you how I feel. But first we must act. We can't just stand here doing nothing.

Yes we can, I explained.

I'll be right back, said Goliath Brigadoon. My feelings will have to wait.

He clutched a knife in his teeth and began shimmying up

the crease in my doppelganger's pants. Proportionally, the crease was crisp, razor sharp, and exact, but in reality Goliath Brigadoon had trouble stretching his arms and legs around it. I watched him go. When he was out of sight, I rested on the floor of the Grand Canyon and pondered my philosophical ideas, eager to observe just how big a thing would have to get before it ceased to exist in any pragmatic way.

Six months later the giant reproduction of my head fell to earth, resulting in vibrations that destroyed a number of important cities. I took a step back for a good look at the big head.

Now I know what I'll look like when I'm dead, I said aloud. Weird. I mean, it's weird to know, not that I look weird. Look at that face in repose. At my funeral everybody's going to be like, That's the best-looking corpse I have ever seen. Like, I would totally go on a date with this dead corpse.

Not long thereafter, Goliath Brigadoon fell to earth as well, suffocated by the molten gold that had spurted from the throat of the robot he had so needlessly decapitated after refusing to heed my theories. The gold had gotten into Goliath Brigadoon's chest cavity, his stomach, his intestines, his eyes, his ears, it had clogged up his mouth and his rectum, it entered the holes where his hair sprouted out, it filled his lungs and his pores, snaked into his veins, his nostrils, the cracks in his heels, invaded his liver and spleen, pushed out and replaced the marrow of his bones, and finally he had burst at the seams.

You silly, wonderful, foolish man, I said. I noted his exquisite tie, now soaked in gold, and considered approvingly his ambitious program of self-improvement. He was a good-looking dude and just my size. I wondered about all the decisions I had ever made.

The body of the supergiant fell across the West.

The whole world rang like a tuning fork. It rained hawks, eagles, and condors, murdered in mid-flight. The oceans jumped from their beds and scorched the plantations with salt. Wild horses ran out of their skins, and their muscle-clad skeletons kept running. The aurora borealis turned ashen. It got as cold as the moon.

The world had been knocked away from the sun. I knew I was the last living thing.

I decided to do what I had vowed never to do again: eat beans. I walked the breadth of the dead earth, gathering cans of beans from the ruins of every nation. Field peas with okra, mung beans, fava, haba, the winged bean and the horse gram, the yam bean and the dow gauk. Refried beans from Guadalajara and baked ones from Boston. Beans of scarlet, green, black, and purple. Fermented, prepared with pork, coated with wasabi, soaked in vinegar, or plain. All the canned beans of all the decimated peoples.

With my immense store of beans straining at several large fishing nets, I waded onshore at the site of the caved-in Sydney Opera House, the exact spot, as I had figured, where a great explosion could, like a booster rocket, thrust our vessel back onto her proper course. That way, conditions would be right for life to evolve again. I thought that would be neat.

And so I partook of every last remaining bean and held deep inside me, with no more outward evidence than a single trembling teardrop, the terrible effects of digestive discomfort.

And so I turned my buttocks toward the heavens.

I was thinking, How about that dude who invented tin cans? He is okay in my book. I couldn't have done this without him. I salute you, dude who invented tin cans.

And there came forth such a burst of methane as has never been known in the history of the galaxy. The stars wavered and dimmed in its wake. The Australian continent broke into a million pieces and sank beneath the waves.

It was warming up, so it seemed that my plan had worked, but new life would take billions of years to evolve, and I wasn't sure I'd be around that long. I admit to entertaining negative thoughts such as, I think I smell like instant potatoes for some reason but there's nobody around to tell me.

I went back to the Grand Canyon and comforted myself by studying the huge and startling likeness of my head.

I don't know what kind of weird animals are going to pop out of the ooze billions of years from now, I said aloud. Maybe I won't even be around by then. But I think it's neat that they'll see this big head with my face on it and be like, What the heck is this? This thing must be like a god or something. Let's make this dude our standard of beauty. Let's totally worship this awesome head.

Using the porch of the ear as a toehold, I climbed up along the sideburn to the scalp. My derby looked as small as a fleck of dandruff there. I lifted it up. She was sitting underneath with her black thong showing, and the veins in her aging legs.

Long time no see, said Glorious Jones.

What were you doing under there?

The process of grieving.

That's understandable.

May I ask why you sent a giant robot of yourself to crash my husband's wake? Or would that be tacky?

Baby, I love your tart tongue, I said.

Seriously, why are you here? she said.

I couldn't tell her the truth about Jimmy.

I found those objects, I said. I wanted to show you.

Objects? Oh, that. That's stupid. Don't bother with that. I was just blowing off steam.

No, but I found them. They're over on the other side of the Grand Canyon if you want to take a walk.

Seriously, don't worry about that. It's not necessary. I hope you didn't spend a lot of time on it.

I helped Glorious Jones down from the head. As we strolled along, I explained about the end of the world, leaving out the part about Jimmy. I told her how the remarkable properties of my admirable derby had saved her life during the global climate change and how, as a result, we were the last two people on earth.

She let it sink in. Finally she said that she thought my hair had gotten bushy.

We had come to the spot where the things I had found for her were scattered in the dust.

Oh brother, she said. This looks like shit. What, you couldn't put them together in a nice way? Where's the four-leaf clover?

I guess it must have blown away during the end of the world, I said.

Where's the hen's tooth?

That wasn't on the list, I said.

I know it was. I should know what was on a list I made

myself. I remember putting it on there, because I was thinking about that saying, the one about hen's teeth. And I was like, I should put that on the list.

Well, you must have forgotten.

I didn't forget.

You had it in your mind but you never wrote it down, probably.

I WROTE IT DOWN, said Glorious Jones.

I twiddled with my derby.

For God's sake, she said. Do you have to keep fidgeting with that? Just put it on your head and stop fooling around. You're driving me insane.

I guess I've been nervous about putting it on. It feels weird to be near it again. I've been missing it for so long, and thinking about it all the time, and here it is, and suddenly I don't know what to do.

That's stupid, said Glorious Jones. It's a hat. Put it on.

I tried to do as she asked, but my derby didn't fit.

I told you your hair was bushy, said Glorious Jones.

She laughed. That was nice.

Hold still, she said.

Glorious Jones scrambled up a crag and shimmied to the end of a ponderosa pine that was growing almost perpendicular to the canyon floor. Sometimes she shimmied with just one hand so she could hold her floppy widow's hat in place.

Watch out, Glorious Jones!

Head down, she said.

She let go of the tree, dropped sixty feet, and landed on the crown of my derby, driving it a little farther onto my head. She slid down the crown and started dancing around the brim, pushing it down.

It still isn't right, I said.

Don't be a crybaby, said Glorious Jones. Okay. I think I'm going to have to stay in one spot and just rub up and down on it. Oh. Oh, oh. How's that? Oh.

By the grace of her exertions my derby moved into place, snug as skin.

The powers of the universe riveted my body. A substance like spun sugar shot in mighty cataracts from my eyes, nostrils, ears, and mouth, and covered the land in a fine and all-encompassing frost. Everywhere it landed, some form of life shot up, a baby deer, an orchid. A little bit landed on Glorious Jones, and she swallowed some of it by mistake, and turned young again.

So

We walked around in the world. Raccoons came up to us. We saw cotton and corn and date trees and an octopus.

This is a sign, said Glorious Jones. Looks like you made everything but people. We should just go ahead and clone everybody and get things up and running again ahead of schedule.

You haven't changed, Glorious Jones. You should know better than to talk about signs. There are no signs. There are only physical facts. Remember when I got you a crystal ball for your birthday? It was gag gift. But then one day I came home unexpectedly and found you descrying in just your panties. That was back during the period when your hair looked like a mushroom cloud. Yes, given certain anomalies in my metabolism and so forth, something unusual recently took place. And yes, the results did some good for the ecosystem, but that was a minor side effect requiring more study.

I still say we should start cloning ASAP.

But baby, I am a robot maker, not a biologist.

While we were apart I was studying biology almost the whole entire time, said Glorious Jones.

I sang "Maybe I'm Amazed" by Paul McCartney because words alone could not express what I felt about the stick-to-itiveness of Glorious Jones.

It took us a while, but we cloned just about everybody, even the people who had gotten killed collaterally on my many recent adventures. And from the bounty of the earth we made bricks and steel and stuff like that and erected nice buildings. When we got done, the earth was just the way it had been before and all the clones were taken out of suspended animation and placed in their cars or cubicles. We put the feral cats out by the Dumpsters and the monkeys in the zoos and nobody even knew they had previously been dead, and that's the earth you're living on today.

When we were done putting everything back in order I looked at Glorious Jones and said, Glorious Jones, you're really something special. I wanted to stop with America because I got tired, and you were like, No way, man. We gotta do the whole freaking earth. We even put Australia back together like a jigsaw puzzle, which is just the sort of fun activity I always wanted to do with you but I was always too busy with my work. We never painted Easter eggs and I always regretted that. I love your idealism, baby. Like when you said, What about the poor people? And I was like, What about them? And you were like, Can't we make them less poor this time? And I was like, I don't know about that, baby. Can't they pull themselves up by their own bootstraps? And you made some excellent points to the contrary, which I can't recall. So finally I talked you out of it due to the concept of free will. And then you were like, What about food? Can't we take some food from where there's a lot of food and put some of it where there's not any? I'm paraphrasing. And I was like, Baby, you're too much. And I had a good laugh at your expense. Let's do something we should have done a long time ago. Get married. This time I'm going to make it stick. Listen, by sucking on my hormones through this incision under my arm I think you can turn big, like me. It hasn't been tested on humans, just a roadrunner, but I say we give it a go.

Not so fast, said Glorious Jones. You were absolutely right about pestilence. We have to go back to the way it was before all this started, when we were complete strangers. The world has to be exactly the same rotten way it was. When I come upstairs and complain about your Alpine bells, you have to act like I'm just another gal.

But this time when we get married I'll act nice.

No. I have to meet Pendleton again. I have to have my children again. I couldn't live without them. Why do you think we stopped cloning people who had been born after a certain point, and burned up the subsequent birth certificates?

I thought it was to save time.

No, Awesome. We're going back to a specific point in human history. I couldn't force myself to clone my own little Abelard and bucktoothed Liza Jane. Even the notion of it felt obscene. I have to bear them again, the natural way. It's my purpose in this world. It's why I was spared. My art degree proved surprisingly useless. As I never tire of mentioning to childless people, having kids really changes your perspective on things. As someone who's not a parent, you could never understand. Look, when your junk splattered on me I turned young as shit. That has to be a sign.

It's wrong to look for signs in scientific phenomena, I reminded her again.

I don't care. We're going back in time. It's all set up. Didn't you notice how we didn't restore any late-model cars?

Glorious Jones got a serious look on her face. Her eyes screwed up with portent and became adorable. You'll have to break my heart again, she said. Break it hard. You'll have to do everything the same, say everything the same, and so will I. You'll vote for the same candidates and eat the same meals. Lose the same amount of money at baccarat. Find all that stupid meaningless shit on that bogus list again. Your life will be nothing but a checklist of meaningless chores, but you can never let on it's all a show, even when we're alone together and no one is watching. Think you can handle it?

I only have the greatest memory ever.

Good. Because as far as I can tell we'll have to repeat the pattern over and over, infinitely.

Wow, I said. That's a big commitment. That's actually like bigger than marriage.

If it helps you to think so, she said. Me, I believe it's an eternal punishment. Every time I see someone with a bad case of rickets or their hands taken off in a war I'm going to know it's because I had to have these certain children and raise them in a certain style.

Baby, you worry too much, I said.

Inside I was thinking about how her children were really my children, but I could never tell her. And how the man she loved was just some dumb robot I had invented.

But I blew on the clouds in a certain way, and stirred the waters of the earth with my giant fingers to duplicate the weather systems that had passed before.

Well, you've been a great sport about everything, said Glorious Jones.

She lifted her veil and waved a black handkerchief in the air, a signal. An ambulance pulled up and the driver got out and opened the back door with a flourish and I could see my wiener in there, resting on a cot.

Charles G. Steffen

ABOUT THE AUTHOR

Jack Pendarvis was the 2007-2008 John and Renee Grisham
Visiting Writer in Residence at the University of Mississippi.
He is a contributing writer to the *Oxford American*, and his
work has also appeared in the *Believer*, the *New York Times
Book Review*, and elsewhere. *Awesome* is his first novel and
his third published book.